Susan Napier

MISTRESS FOR A
WEEKEND

MISTRESS
To A
MILLIONAIRE

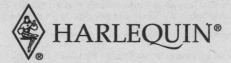

D0036143

HARLEQUIN®

TORONTO • NEW YORK • LONDON
AMSTERDAM • PARIS • SYDNEY • HAMBURG
STOCKHOLM • ATHENS • TOKYO • MILAN • MADRID
PRAGUE • WARSAW • BUDAPEST • AUCKLAND

ISBN-13: 978-0-373-12569-2
ISBN-10:   0-373-12569-0

MISTRESS FOR A WEEKEND

First North American Publication 2006.

Copyright © 2006 by Susan Napier.

www.eHarlequin.com

Printed in U.S.A.

HARLEQUIN® Presents

Take a look at our books for September!

A marriage ended or a marriage mended? Kayla has been bought back by her estranged husband, billionaire Duardo Alvarez, in Helen Bianchin's scorcher *Purchased by the Billionaire*. Bedded for revenge or wedded for passion? Freya has made the mistake of hiding the existence of Italian Enrico Ranieri's little son, and she must make amends as his convenient wife in Michelle Reid's torrid tale *The Ranieri Bride*. Is revenge sweet? Greek tycoon Christos Carides certainly thinks so when he seduces Becca Summer in Kim Lawrence's sizzling story, *The Carides Pregnancy*. But for how long? Out for the count? Italian aristocrat Alessio Ramontella certainly thinks he's KO'd innocent English beauty Laura, but will she actually succumb to his ruthless seduction? Find out in *The Count's Blackmail Bargain* by Sara Craven. Meantime, Carol Marinelli's mixing business with intense pleasure in her new UNCUT novel, *Taken for His Pleasure*. It's a gold band of blackmail for temporary bride Maddison as she's forced to marry wealthy Greek Demetrius Papasakis in *The Greek's Convenient Wife* by Melanie Milburne. Mistress material? Nora Lang doesn't think she's got what it takes in Susan Napier's *Mistress for a Weekend*. But tycoon Blake MacLeod thinks Nora definitely has something special—confidential information. And he'll keep her in his bed to prevent her giving it away. Finally, an ultimatum...*The Marriage Ultimatum* by Helen Brooks. It's Carter Blake's only option when Liberty refuses to let him take her.

MISTRESS
TO A
MILLIONAIRE

*She's his in the bedroom,
but he can't buy her love…*

Showered with diamonds, draped in
exquisite lingerie, whisked around the
world in the lap of luxury…

The ultimate fantasy becomes
a reality in Harlequin Presents.

Live the dream with more
MISTRESS TO A MILLIONAIRE
titles by your favorite authors.

Coming in November:

The Mediterranean Millionaire's Mistress
by Maggie Cox
#2584

All about the author...
Susan Napier

SUSAN NAPIER is a former journalist and
scriptwriter who turned to writing romance
fiction after her two sons were born. She lives
in Auckland, New Zealand, with her journalist
husband, who generously provides the ongoing
inspiration for her fictional heroes, and two
temperamental cats whose curious paws
contribute the occasional typographical error
when they join her at the keyboard.

Born on St. Valentine's Day, Susan feels that it was
her destiny to write romances, and having written
over thirty books for Harlequin she still loves the
challenges of working within the genre. She likes
writing traditional tales with a twist, and believes
that to keep romance alive you have to keep the
faith—to believe in love. Not just in the romantic
kind of love that pervades her books, but in the
everyday caring-and-sharing kind of love that
builds enduring relationships.

Susan's extended family is scattered over the
globe, which is fortunate as she enjoys traveling
and seeking out new experiences to fuel her
flights of imagination.

Susan loves to hear from readers and can be
contacted by e-mail through the Web site at
www.harlequinpresents.com.

In memory of my dad,
the little guy with the big smile.

CHAPTER ONE

BLAKE MACLEOD had been watching the young woman for some time before she became aware of his presence.

At first it had merely been out of idle curiosity. He'd happened to be glancing her way when she had tottered out of the lift and his attention had been caught by the paleness of her freckled face in the wash of the overhead light, and the abruptness with which she had halted, regarding the revolving floor of the restaurant with ill-concealed dismay. Her teeth had dug deep into her lower lip as her gaze resolutely avoided the circular sweep of floor-to-ceiling windows revealing the lights of the rain-washed city twinkling far below, fastening instead on the metal joints in the carpet where the fixed central column of Auckland's Sky Tower became the slowly rotating platform which formed the main body of the restaurant.

In any other circumstances Blake probably wouldn't have given the unprepossessing lone female a second glance, but he had been feeling dangerously bored and ripe for any form of distraction. He had only attended the party under pressure, as a courtesy to his host, a valued business client, and he was already calculating the earliest he could leave without giving offence. Once he would have relished the opportunity to rub shoulders with a room full of movers-and-shakers, but at thirty-three he was well past the stage where he felt the need to impress.

From his vantage point by one of the seamless windows, he had studied the latecomer over the heads of the party-goers as she hovered uncertainly in the elevated reception area, a folded umbrella clutched to her chest in a white-knuckled grip, her figure shrouded by the damp folds of a vo-luminous brown raincoat. She stood out from the colourful crowd like an ordinary house sparrow amidst a pride of peacocks. Her hair was a nimbus of brown curls frothing out around the blanched oval of her face and Blake guessed that, her style of coiffure notwithstanding, she had found the ride in the glass-fronted lift a hair-raising experience.

Tuning out the sycophantic conversation of his compan-ions, Blake speculated on the reason for the sparrow's shell-shocked state. He could eliminate the theory that she was a gatecrasher afraid of being caught—she never would have got past the tight security at the base of the Sky Tower if she hadn't had an invitation. The most obvious answer to her angst was that she had a fear of heights, but if that was the case why on earth would she have accepted an invitation to a party atop the tallest tower in the southern hemisphere?

One of the restaurant hostesses on cloakroom duty ap-proached her, and the twin brackets around Blake's hard mouth deepened in amusement as he watched the sparrow erupt into a flurry of awkward movements, getting both the umbrella and a large black-beaded evening bag entangled in the sleeves of the raincoat in her haste to shed her outer plumage. By the time she had freed herself from the bunched fabric, and picked up the umbrella and bag she had dropped in the process, her pale face was flushed with embarrass-ment. She thrust the trailing coat and umbrella apologeti-cally at the bemused hostess and walked jerkily towards the short flight of steps that led down to the fan of tables, tucking the beaded clutch bag into the crook of her elbow as she surveyed the glittering throng with a glazed expression that contained a curious combination of desperation and determi-nation.

Blake nearly choked on his drink when he saw the dress she had been hiding under the brown shroud. It was a plain black strapless number, blatantly sexy and sophisticated—and it didn't suit her at all. Rather than enhancing her femininity, it merely emphasised her flaws—making her bare freckled shoulders appear too wide and the rest of her body look too boyishly straight. Instead of smouldering sensuality, she projected all angles and elbows, her face looking oddly naked in spite of—or perhaps because of—her heavily made-up eyes. She was quite tall and therefore correspondingly leggy, but the hem of her dress finished too far below her knees to showcase what Blake suspected were her best assets. As she teetered down the staircase in shiny spiked heels, still nibbling at her pale pink lower lip, he thought she looked more like a fresh-scrubbed, freckle-faced kid playing dress-up, and from the way she kept discreetly hitching at the outer edges of the strapless bodice she felt no more comfortable than she looked.

Not his type at all, he thought wryly, as he watched her reach the bottom of the stairs and grab a wineglass from the nearest tray, sending the adjacent glasses skittering with her straying forearm and almost upending the entire silver platter down the waiter's impeccable white jacket. Her flustered apologies were accepted with a pained smile and her exposed skin was again bright pink as she attempted to melt inconspicuously into the crowd.

Blake got the impression that she spent a great deal of her time apologising.

Most *definitely* not his type.

Blake's taste in female companions ran to genuine sophisticates: beautiful, self-confident, worldly women who craved attention rather than interest, who never involved themselves in embarrassing situations—physical or emotional. Women who might tax his ingenuity in bed but who rarely challenged his independence, and who could be relied upon to accept an amicable parting of the ways when the affair had run its course.

Inexplicably, the downy-haired sparrow continued to bob

in and out of his wandering attention over the next half-hour. At just over six foot, Blake had a reasonably unobstructed view over the heads of most of the crowd and, since her high heels made her almost his equal in height, it was easy to find her at a glance. He noticed that, unlike everyone else, she stayed well away from the windows, barely moving from the spot where she had come in, quaffing the free-flowing wine as she studied the passing parade of guests.

Even from a distance he could see the tension in the set of her shoulders, the aura of suppressed energy that gave her brooding watchfulness a sense of purpose. She seemed poised to take wing at any moment—but for flight or fight? What was it she was searching for amongst the crowd? Someone to rescue her from her fear? Blake mocked his own whimsy as he turned back to field the conversational ball that was tossed his way. The answer was probably far more prosaic, and she was simply looking for someone she'd arranged to meet at the party.

The next time he glanced her way she was scooting forward to intercept another roving waiter, swapping her empty glass for a brimming champagne flute. Blake unconsciously held his breath until she safely negotiated the exchange, then watched in fatalistic fascination as she stepped back on to a portly matron's foot and spun around in dismay, elbowing her victim's unfortunate escort sharply in the solar plexus and dripping wine on his shoes. Recognising the head of a powerful quasi-Government think-tank on foreign trade, Blake winced...although, come to think of it, there'd been a time or two during the industry consulting process when he'd been tempted to take a slug at the pompous little windbag himself.

Perhaps the sparrow was the embodiment of his cosmic revenge! he thought, a slight smile curving his hard mouth as he looked down into the melting remains of his Scotch on the rocks. Unfortunately, the ambitious young businesswoman at his side who had been uttering flirtatious remarks took it as a sign of encouragement, and he was forced to adopt a brutal uninterest to convince her that she was mistaken.

When he looked up again it was to discover with a mild jolt of disappointment that his idle entertainment for the evening had disappeared. He turned his head and suddenly found himself staring straight into the brooding eyes of his former quarry. She had edged out of her comfort zone and was with a cluster of people helping themselves to canapés from one of the second-tier tables, close enough for him to see that he might have been wrong about her legs being her best asset. Her wide-set kohl-lined eyes were the sensuous colour of old gold, glowing with burnished brightness under their heavy-smudged green lids, dominating her otherwise unremarkable face. And they were currently trained on Blake with an arrested intensity. Big, luminous, disturbingly warm eyes, fringed with thickly coated black lashes; siren's eyes, that seemed to look straight through his polished shield of cynical sophistication into the hidden secrets of his soul.

To his astonishment Blake felt his body suffuse with heat, as if all his secrets had suddenly become X-rated. He gritted his teeth in disbelief as he felt the blood rising to his face, fighting to keep his expression impassive under that steadfast golden stare.

A clumsy freckle-faced kid was making him blush, for God's sake!

He shifted abruptly, using a comment addressed to him as an excuse to turn his back, but his mind was distracted by the disquieting realisation that he had, in effect, blinked first. He, who had never backed away from a challenge, who had outfaced kings of industry and princes of wealth, had flinched from a confrontation with a mere girl. Or was it himself he was unwilling to confront…and the underlying reason for his growing boredom with occasions like these?

Without turning around, he knew that he was still under surveillance, still being assessed by those golden eyes…but assessed for what?

The short hairs on the back of his neck began to prickle. A sure sign of impending trouble. Fortunately, he and trouble were intimate acquaintances. Handling strife was his chief talent and major occupation.

And the most important thing he had learned over the years was that it was far safer to meet the arrival of trouble head-on than to ignore it and hope it would leave you alone.

CHAPTER TWO

ELEANOR LANG'S fingers tightened around her wineglass as she made another visual sweep of the restaurant to check that she hadn't overlooked anyone.

Her eyes skipped impatiently over a face which could have belonged to a male model. She wasn't looking for the most handsome man in the room, nor even the most charming. She had discounted men who were obviously with their wives or significant others, which cut the field down considerably, and ignored the fun-loving party animals. She wasn't after character or personality, kindness or courtesy.

No, what Nora was looking for was much rarer. What she wanted was the most *dangerous* man in the room.

Her eyes returned to the broad shoulders which she had been studying a few moments before…the long, straight back encased in the faultless perfection of a tailormade suit. The man with the fierce grey eyes.

Blake MacLeod.

She hadn't known who he was when she had first caught a glimpse of his trademark scowl, but what she saw had made her spine tingle. She had immediately shifted closer to get a better look, squeezing her way over to the table of food which was directly across from the loose cluster of people around him.

Whoever he was, he certainly didn't look *safe*. In fact, he looked as surly as the devil and bored to within an inch of his life. One hand was thrust into his trouser pocket, ruffling the unbuttoned jacket of his light grey suit, the other lifting a squat glass of whisky to his mouth as he stared stonily over the rim at the attractive woman beside him, blatant disdain for whatever she was saying plastered across his harsh features. His collar-length hair was as black as sin, sleeked back to reveal a prominent forehead and thick black brows that gave the impression of a permanent frown riding astride his hawkish nose. He couldn't be classed as handsome but he was fully mature and formidably masculine. His face was long and narrow, his cheeks hollowed beneath jutting cheek-bones, and there was already a dark shadow blooming along the unforgiving line of his smooth-shaven jaw.

All in all, he looked lean, mean and hungry. The kind of man who would sell his own grandmother if it would turn him a profit, and give no quarter in a fight.

Not that Nora had any intention of fighting him! On the contrary…

Then their eyes had unexpectedly met, and she'd felt the same scary sensation that she had experienced coming up in the lift. Adrenaline pumped through her veins and sucked the blood from her head to fuel her racing heart.

Her first impulse was to pretend that she just happened to be casually glancing around, but she was forced to brazen it out when she found that she couldn't look away, fascinated by the molten flare of acknowledgement in his silvery eyes before they rapidly chilled to the colour of tempered grey steel. Curiosity unfurled inside her, spiked with a delicious thrill of fear at her own daring.

They must have stared at each other for only a second or two, but to Nora it seemed like aeons. When he finally turned away she went limp, and realised that during those few moments of suspended animation every major muscle in her body had contracted to a state of red alert.

She stiffened her wobbly knees, congratulating herself on her boldness. Danger Man knew she existed. For a split second she had forced him to notice her. That was a start, wasn't it?

Face it, Nora, you're not the sort of woman that men notice.

Her stomach clenched as she pushed away the intruding voice, reminding her that she hadn't had anything to eat since breakfast, her lunch break having been spent shopping for the elegant but annoyingly uncomfortable dress she was wearing. She tugged uneasily at the top of the low-cut bodice to make sure that it hadn't drifted down again. She didn't think she had enough cleavage to do justice to the style but Ryan had insisted that she wear something black and strapless, which he thought was the ultimate in feminine sophistication, to tonight's party.

He had given her some money and told her to buy a new dress for herself after work, but she had been so eager to make him proud of her that she had squeezed the task into a shortened lunch break and worked like a maniac all afternoon so that she could leave early and rush home to try and pamper herself into the semblance of a glamour girl.

She had been such a gullible idiot, she thought, her throat tightening at the memory of the ghastly scene that had ensued at her flat. Her friends often chided her for being too trusting, and now she had wrenching proof that they had been right. Because it would never have occurred to *her* to be unfaithful, she had actually been pleased that Ryan seemed to be getting on so well with her young and trendy new flatmate.

A sudden stinging in her eyes threatened to ruin the make-up Nora had carefully applied to conceal her tear-swollen tissues. To think that she had naively imagined Ryan's unaccustomed generosity over the dress had meant that he wanted to make the evening *really* special for her—maybe he was planning to suggest that they move in together! Instead, it had been a sop to his guilty conscience. She was only twenty-five and already she knew what it was like to be dumped for a younger model!

Anger boiled up like hot lava inside her, scalding away any

remaining urge to cry. She snatched up a succulent pink prawn from the table in front of her and bit it viciously in half. She had wasted five years of her life trying to mould herself into the kind of woman she thought Ryan could love. From now she was going to be her *own* woman. Starting tonight, she was going to prove that everything that Ryan had said about her was a self-serving lie!

A man likes a woman to take the initiative sometimes. But you're such a mouse when it comes to new experiences. At least Kelly knows how to have fun. You never want to experiment or take any risks....

Nora smouldered over the humiliating words that he had thrown at her as she had blundered her way out of the flat, numbed by the icy shock of his betrayal. He had been flattered by her feelings for him, but he had never meant them to tie him down. He was sure that if she looked around she would eventually find someone more compatible....

No one as fascinating as Ryan Trent, of course. No doubt he expected her to hook up with a man who was as timid and boring as herself!

Her eyes had remained trained on the man who looked like the absolute antithesis of all those things.

'Do you know who that is over there?' she asked a stock-broker acquaintance who was fishing in the same platter of prawns. 'The tall, dark man with the killer frown.'

The woman followed her sight-line and practically shivered when she said his name.

Blake MacLeod.

Ryan might accuse her of being more interested in computers than people, but even Nora had heard of Blake MacLeod...vaguely.

She remembered someone in the office reading aloud from a newspaper column about New Zealand's biggest domestically owned transport and communications conglomerate. Much of its current strong growth had been credited to the 'defiantly unpolished' MacLeod, who was said to be ferociously hard-working and ice-cool under pressure. He had been described as a maverick for his unorthodox views on business, and a brilliant opportunist for his ruthless, take-no-prisoners approach to acquiring ailing competitors. Much had been made of his working-class background, lack of formal qualifications and his cynical disrespect for the financial establishment.

He was also, she dredged up from the blurred fringes of her recall, an unrepentant bachelor.

'Isn't he the head of PresCorp?'

'Not yet. He's Prescott Williams's chief troubleshooter, but rumour has it that when the old man retires or kicks the bucket, the whole kit-and-caboodle will land fair and square in his lap,' her informant supplied obligingly. 'All the PresCorp shares are under Williams's thumb, but he never married and there aren't any children to inherit, you see.' She leaned closer and lowered her voice. 'MacLeod hadn't even graduated from high school when Williams took him into the firm and made him his pet protégé. Some say it's because he's really the old man's illegitimate son....'

Nora wasn't interested in his murky antecedents, only his current personal status. 'Does he have a girlfriend?'

The broker gave Nora's pale, absorbed face a sidelong look. 'You want to steer clear of the likes of him,' she warned kindly. 'He's got a bad reputation with women—great in the sack, but an ice-man out of it. Acquires mistresses rather than lovers, and none of them last longer than a couple of months. "Use 'em and lose 'em" seems to be his motto.'

In other words, he was every bit as dangerous as he looked. Perfect!

'He's not your type, anyway, Nora,' the other woman added as a parting shot. 'His women are all interchangeably gorgeous—and definitely not the kind to take home to Mother, if you know what I mean....'

She meant that Nora wasn't *his* type. No one had ever

come even close to calling her gorgeous. The words that had haunted her all evening rang again in her ears:

I'm sorry, Nora, but you must know this was inevitable. I mean—you've been a good mate but, let's face it, the sex between us has always been pretty pedestrian, hasn't it? You take ages to get heated up and then you're only lukewarm. I'm not blaming you—some women are like that—but I need someone who physically excites me....

As an apology it had been a slap in the face. So he wasn't blaming her for being stodgy and undersexed—how kind of him! She'd been a virgin when she met Ryan, so how had she been supposed to know that 'the sex' was *pedestrian*? She had never looked upon it as having sex, anyway, she had quaintly imagined that they were making love, sharing more than just their bodies. And he had never given any indication that he was dissatisfied with her lovemaking...or her cooking, or her frequent ironing of his shirts and tidying of his apartment, or the amount of unpaid time she had spent after-hours at Maitlands Consulting, where they both worked, helping him meet his project deadlines.

Blake MacLeod might be a 'user' but at least he was open about it.

And he was 'great in the sack'.

Nora was engulfed by a wave of heat. What she was contemplating was sheer madness, but she had earned the right to go a little crazy. She was tired of people pointing out her limitations. She had nothing to lose and everything to gain.

After all, what was the very worst that could happen if she went over and tried out her womanly wiles on Blake MacLeod? An embarrassing snub? Nora was living proof that no one ever died of humiliation.

On the other hand, in the wilder realms of possibility, if she actually succeeded...

Her imagination failed her, and Nora took a hasty gulp of her drink to bolster her courage. She could do this. She might not be beautiful but she was smart—smarter, in fact, than

Ryan, although she had learnt to downplay the fact when they were in company.

If only he wasn't standing next to a window….

'Those who are about to die, salute you,' she muttered, raising her glass in a fatalistic toast before forging her way through the crowd.

A passing waitress mistook her gesture for a request for another drink and Nora paused to accept her offer of a refill. She had a feeling that she might need it!

Progress in her spindly five-inch heels was slow, but given their inherent instability she didn't dare hurry for fear of twisting an ankle.

The nearer she got to that lean imposing back, the greater the number of butterflies trapped inside her chest. Her palms went clammy and her breath shortened. With every step she became more aware of the vast expanse of glass beyond him, and the fact that at any moment the dizzying vista could open up beneath her feet. Only by focusing fiercely on the solid breadth of his shoulders could she block out the incipient panic, and by the time she fetched up behind him she was wound as tight as a drum.

At the last moment, with her hand reaching out to tap him on the shoulder and what she hoped was a mysterious Mona Lisa smile pinned to her lips, her nerve failed.

She jerked her hand back and wheeled away, but the sharp movement dislodged the clutch-bag wedged under her armpit and it thudded to the floor, the faulty catch springing open to disgorge the contents.

'Oh, no!' Nora sank down on her knees amongst the forest of legs, trying to hold her wineglass on an even keel as she started to rake her possessions back into the yawning maw of the capacious bag with her other hand. To her mortification a floral-wrapped tampon had rolled up against the swivelling toe of a highly polished masculine shoe. She swept it up in her palm and thrust it into the dark recesses of her bag as the shoe flexed and the owner came down in a crouch beside her.

'Allow me…' Blake MacLeod's amused grey eyes met her horrified ones as he picked up a pair of low-heeled black velvet shoes wedged one inside the other, and handed them to her.

'You carry an extra pair of shoes in your handbag?' he said, under cover of the party noise which buzzed uninterrupted over their heads.

His voice was a deep, soft drawl that sent sensual ripples across Nora's exposed nerves.

'They're for driving,' she said quickly, avoiding his gaze as she stuffed them awkwardly into the bag. Thank goodness he had politely ignored the tampon!

'Really?'

Sensitised by her agonised embarrassment, she was quick to detect the lilt of scepticism. God, she was such a terrible liar. Why did she even bother?

'No, not really,' she confessed helplessly, sinking down on her folded legs. 'I—that is, I bought the ones I'm wearing on the way to the party.' She couldn't believe that he had actually stooped to help her. Was this fate's reward, or punishment, for her moment of cowardice? 'At the hotel boutique downstairs. I was passing and saw them in the window and, well…'

He tipped his head to look down at her feet, tucked beneath her bottom, and blinked, his hard mouth kicking up, revealing the unexpected fullness of his lower lip. 'Let me guess—you just *had* to have them….'

He made her sound wickedly self-indulgent, used to the instant gratification of her impulsive desires.

'Something like that,' she agreed vaguely.

Because Ryan was slightly shorter than her five-foot-nine, and unduly sensitive about it, Nora hadn't possessed any high heels…until tonight. She had been wandering through the complex, following the signs from the underground car park to the Sky Tower lifts, when she had spotted the frivolous, tall strappy pair she was now wearing in the glitzy boutique window…shoes that would have made Ryan look like a tiny insignificant speck beside her. She had immediately marched in and bought them. Only a vestige of her normal thrift had restrained her from binning her low-heeled pumps.

'I admire a woman who knows exactly what she wants... and goes after it,' he murmured, rescuing more of her scattered possessions from under passing feet.

She was perversely annoyed by his approval, the rage simmering just beneath the surface of her skin unconsciously seeking an outlet.

'Instead of expecting a man to get it for her, you mean?' she challenged, startled to hear that her voice was husky with suppressed temper. Heavens! She actually sounded provocative.

'Something like that.' He smiled, tossing her own phrase back at her, and she was swamped by a hot bloom of physical awareness. His eyes drifted lower, to the ginger-flecked expanse of skin that rose above the flattened curve of her bodice, and the speculative gleam that she glimpsed through his thick lashes made her nervously check the security of her dress with a discreet upward tug under one arm. His white teeth flashed as he innocently returned his gaze to her rosy countenance.

The fully fledged smile did fascinating things to his sullen face, warming the cold angles and austere planes and lending his mouth a sensuous softness. Close up, she could see the smooth grain of his olive skin, darkened further by the kiss of summer sun and the blue-black shadow on his chin and upper lip. She discovered that his deep-set eyes had tiny chips of green in them, hidden gems embedded in the grey sheetrock, flecks of emerald fire that sparked in her a sudden lust for precious stones. When she inhaled she found that she was breathing in the spicy scent of his body, not an artificially astringent cologne, expensive and anonymous, but his own unique natural fragrance—musky and unmistakably male....

'You certainly seem to have the knack of acquiring things,' he was saying, helping her to gather up her notebook and calculator, wallet, eye-make-up compact, tissues, vial of perfume, keys, pen-knife, a card of fuse-wire, mini-torch, nail file, comb, travel toothbrush, hotel sewing kit and tube of breath mints amongst sundry other bits and pieces. Pivoting from his splayed crouch he had the greater reach, occasionally stretching across her, the sleeve of his jacket brushing goose-pimples along Nora's bare arm.

'I— Really, you've helped enough. I can manage the rest myself,' she protested, trying to distract his fascinated attention from the embarrassing amount of personal clutter. She saw him flipping through a small folder of family photos and snatched it away as he reached the image of herself as a plump, fuzzy-haired teenager.

'That was taken when I was sixteen,' she couldn't help saying.

'You don't look much older than that now.'

'Is that supposed to be a compliment?'

'Most women enjoy giving the impression they're younger than their years,' he said, making her feel unutterably gauche.

'It's the freckles,' she sighed. 'They make me look like a perpetual schoolgirl.'

He picked up her blood donor card. By the time he had finished 'helping' her, Nora thought, she would be totally stripped of all mystery. 'Please, don't let me keep you from your conversation with your friends—'

'This is much more interesting,' he drawled, with the teasing inflection which made her feel hot and edgy. 'And I always finish what I start. It's sort of a trademark of mine. Besides, they're acquaintances, not friends. My friends know better than to bore me.'

'What happens when you're bored?' she dared to ask.

'I behave like a complete boor,' he said languidly.

'Oh...*Oh*!' A hiccup of startled laughter erupted from Nora as she belatedly recognised his pun, her eyes crinkling into merry crescents. 'The insensitive and ill-mannered person, or the male pig?' she asked with pretended confusion.

'Actually a boar is an *uncastrated* male pig.' He corrected her second option, and watched her eyelashes flutter and her freckles fight against a rising tide of pink. 'I feel that's an important distinction, since my answer is…yes to both.'

'Really?' She wasn't about to let a man get the better of her—not tonight. 'Then you must have a lot of very tolerant friends.'

He laughed. 'Or a few very interesting ones.' He held aloft a yellow-handled tool and shot her a compelling lift of his dark eyebrows. 'A *screwdriver*?'

'I like to be prepared for every eventuality,' she told him, plucking it out of his hand, noticing that his fingers were long and supple and his nails beautifully manicured.

'So I see,' he murmured, as he spied the last stray item, almost hidden by a fold of her dress flaring away from her knee. He handed her the small foil package with grave ceremony.

She stared at it lying on the palm of her hand, stricken by a chilling thought. Thank God she was unable to take oral contraceptives and therefore had had to insist that Ryan always used a condom. What if Kelly wasn't the first woman he had slept with during the year that their relationship had been sexually intimate? She would have been forced to wonder whether her health was at risk.

With a jolt she realised that it had been ages since she and Ryan had actually made love…. He had been away on business, then he had gone on a skiing trip to Colorado with his rugby mates, and after he got back he had been busy with work, or she had, and their social life had got busier. There had always seemed to be a ready enough reason *not* to make love, and Nora admitted that she had barely noticed their extended bout of celibacy—on her side at least!

'It *is* yours, isn't it?' he said, intrigued by the parade of expressions across her abstracted face.

'What? Oh…yes.' She blushed, dropping it hurriedly into her bag. 'But don't let it lead you to jump to any hasty conclusions about me,' she added, putting her drink down carefully on the carpet while she fished about to find the fuse-wire and quickly wound a 15-amp strand in a figure of eight around the worn clasp.

'The only conclusion I've come to is that you're probably a highly organised person in a disorganised kind of way,' he said wryly, watching her complete the makeshift repair with a deft twist of the fragile wire. 'Shall we rejoin the party before people start wondering what we're getting up to down here?' He rose smoothly to his feet, showing no signs of stiffness from his prolonged crouch, whisking away her bag and wineglass and placing them on the edge of the window table behind him, next to his own drink, before stooping to offer both his hands to Nora.

His palms were slightly rough, the friction of his skin sliding against hers producing sparks of heat that fanned hotter as his fingers tightened, totally encompassing her slender hands, making her momentarily feel trapped and helpless and alarmingly vulnerable. A quick flex of his legs and he hauled her upright in one fluid, easy movement. Alarm turned to a rush of unexpected excitement, the sparks leaping from the point of contact to sizzle up Nora's arms and razzle-dazzle around her body with electrifying speed, making it difficult to breathe, let alone coordinate her movements. The force of her forward momentum plastered her against his shirt front and she flailed on her precarious heels to find her balance, gasping when she felt an ominous downward drag on her breasts.

'Oh, stop! Don't move!' she hissed at him as she realised what was happening. 'I think I've caught one of my heels in the hem of my dress!' she groaned, hopping on one wobbly foot like a drunken stork.

He uttered a smothered curse, threaded with laughter, obediently freezing in position.

'This isn't funny!' she whispered fiercely into his ear. 'I'll be topless in a moment if we're not careful.'

'And this would be a bad thing?' he chuckled softly, his breath stirring the silky curls that feathered her cheek. The deep vibration in his chest resonated against her squashed breasts and Nora was mortified to feel them begin to tingle, the nipples budding against the sheer fabric of her strapless bra, the top edge of which was now peeking above the satin band of her bodice.

'*Yes!*' Her chin was level with his shoulder, his tanned throat a tempting few inches from her mouth.

'For goodness' sake, stop laughing at me and try doing something *helpful*,' she gritted. She pulled her hands from his loosening grasp and looked down over her shoulder, arching back to try and unhook her spiked heel from the looped thread, but the twisting motion jerked her awkwardly bent leg and she gave a little squeak as she felt herself begin to pop free from the top of her dress.

Her squeak turned to a breathless gasp as his hands whipped to her sides, palms clamping around the front of her ribs with almost painful force, splayed fingers digging into her back, anchoring the straining fabric firmly in place, her dignity still intact. 'It's all right. I've got you. *Now* try,' he advised.

Nora was aware that she was teetering on the brink of social disaster. She licked her dry lips, her heart still pounding with fright, scarcely able to draw breath against the fierce compression of his grip. She stared up at the man holding her, her eyes wide and dark with doubt, her teeth sinking painfully into her bottom lip. She had already been betrayed by one man tonight. She had picked Blake MacLeod out as a dangerous man…what if it was an element of cruelty in his nature which gave him the dark aura she had found so appealing? What if he was setting her up for fresh humiliation?

'Go ahead—I won't let go.' There wasn't a trace of his previous mockery in his quiet voice and cool gaze. 'Trust me.'

His calmness and the continuing steady pressure around her ribs curbed her fears. In any case, trussed up as she was, she really didn't have any choice *but* to trust him.

It took her several flustered seconds to untangle the transparent thread from her snagged heel, and when she was finally standing on two feet again she uttered a ragged sigh of relief.

She was grateful that he had drawn her slightly away from the group he had been talking to, sparing her the embarrassment of introductions. 'Thank you.'

'My pleasure….'

The silky mockery was back and as their eyes met she was even more aware of his hands still firmly caging her ribs, his thumbs sloping up under her breasts so that with every exhaled breath she stroked herself against him. All he had to do was to alter the angle of his thumbs and he would find the stiff crests which pushed against the shiny satin, she thought hectically. She could feel the long muscles of his thighs bunching as they tensed against hers, the hard thrust of his hips still bracing the centre of her slender body, generating a primitive response that filled her with a furious elation. The social buzz around them faded from her consciousness, her breathing quickening in response to the sultry recognition that darkened his grey eyes. Her heart jumped inside her chest, throbbing against the warm pad of his thumb, and her sensitised skin crackled with energy.

'We haven't even been introduced,' she murmured faintly, having difficulty shaping the words on her thickened tongue.

'It's a little late to be formal. I'm Blake MacLeod.'

'I know.' She saw his eyelids give a wary flicker. 'After I saw you across the room, I wondered who you were, so I asked someone…'

'I see.' The brackets around his mouth relaxed. 'And?'

He obviously sensed there had been more to it than a simple identification. 'She said that you had a bad reputation with women and I should avoid you like the plague.'

'And yet…here you are,' he said in a neutral tone that was at odds with his smouldering eyes. 'Should I have asked someone about *you*?'

A rueful smile revealed Nora's disproportionately wide mouth and splendid teeth. 'It wouldn't have done you much good. I hardly know anyone in this crowd. I only got invited because I used to flat with the sister of the girl who's turning twenty-one.' Her eyes were almost on a level with his and it gave her a powerful kick to look directly into the windows of his deep, dark soul. 'I'm Nora.'

His impressive eyebrows lifted. 'Just Nora?'

'Eleanor, actually, but no one calls me that,' she breezed. No one except Ryan when he was impatient with her— grinding up the syllables in his gritted teeth!

Blake was silent, and she realised that he wasn't going to let her get away with the evasion. So much for hoping that she could cloak herself in alluring mystery for the evening.

'Lang. Nora Lang,' she said, adopting a flippant Bondian drawl. 'Does that make you any the wiser?'

He dipped his head, acknowledging the introduction. 'Not wiser, but certainly better informed. I always try to make informed decisions.'

'How boring,' she teased. 'Don't you like surprises?'

'It depends on the nature of the surprise,' he said, deliberately running his eyes over her captive body.

She felt her skin tighten in every pore. 'Are you always so cautious?'

'It depends on the nature of the threat.'

The verbal fencing was having a heady effect on Nora's battered self-confidence. 'Do I threaten you, Mr MacLeod?' she asked with a sweet smile.

'The idea seems to excite you.'

She felt a sluggish warmth move through her veins. 'I'll admit it has a certain raw appeal...'

'It's an interesting proposition, Nora, but I'm afraid I'm not into S&M.'

She blushed, not pink, but a vivid rose-red. 'I wasn't—I didn't mean *that*!'

'No? Sorry, I must have misunderstood,' he said with such patent insincerity that they both knew he was lying, and mightily enjoying her confusion.

'I'm not into anything weird!' she said firmly.

'How about mildly kinky?'

She thought of Ryan and Kelly in the bathroom. In the *bath* of all places, in the middle of the afternoon. *Nora's* bath! Boring, undemanding, unadventurous Nora who obviously didn't know what she was missing....

'Define kinky.'

He laughed, a deep masculine rumble of appreciation. *'Now* who's being cautious?'

'A woman alone has to take care not to raise expectations she's not prepared to fulfil,' she said primly.

'You're here alone?' In spite of the upward inflexion it was more of a statement than a question, and he didn't wait for an answer. 'I watched you as you came in,' he admitted unexpectedly.

'Did you?' Her smile widened for an instant before she re-membered her ignominious entrance. 'Oh. And I suppose now you think I ricochet about the place like some sort of unguided missile,' she said with a sigh.

His fingers briefly contracted on her ribcage. 'Or perhaps a cleverly guided one.'

'Are you accusing me of dropping my bag at your feet on purpose, in order to meet you?' she demanded, clenching her fists against his chest.

'Did you?'

She tipped her chin and looked down her nose at him. 'That is *so* arrogant! Do you consider yourself so irresistibly attractive that you automatically assume that every woman is grovelling to attract your attention?'

His mouth ticked up at her haughty response. 'Well, not *every* woman. *Did* you?'

'No, of course I didn't!'

Then she recalled her chaotic thoughts in the moments before she had turned coward. 'Well…' She caught her lower lip between her teeth as she struggled with her over-scrupu-lous conscience. 'Maybe I *might* have been thinking of a way to introduce myself, but…no, I wouldn't have—certainly not consciously, anyway…'

His eyes were on that tell-tale worrying of her lip. 'You mean it was in the nature of a Freudian drop?' he said, with such suspicious blandness that her fists relaxed against his chest.

'Is that any different from a Freudian slip?' she asked, discreetly smoothing out a small crease she had made in his yellow silk tie.

'It's generally more revealing,' he told her, and paused before adding, 'Rather like that dress.'

She followed his gaze and uttered a stifled sound of annoyance when she saw that the embroidered edge of her black bra was still visible above the top of her dress. He beat her to the rescue, the backs of his fingers branding her with their searing warmth as they dipped beneath the fabric at the side of her breasts to gently hitch up her top by several freckles.

'Thank you,' she muttered, her hands automatically replacing his as he stepped back, leaving her bereft of his disturbing touch. She wriggled even more securely into the dress while he turned to pick up his neglected drink. 'I wish I'd never worn the wretched thing,' she grumbled. 'I knew it wasn't right for me.'

Unfortunately she'd had no choice since it was what she had been wearing when she had fled the flat. She had been trying on her dress and accessories when she had heard odd noises from the bathroom. Believing Kelly was out on a modelling job, she had snatched up a heavy lamp with which to clock the intruder if he turned nasty. In hindsight, she wished she had used it!

To Nora's chagrin Blake didn't disagree. He tucked her bag in the crook of her elbow and placed her wineglass in her hand. 'So why wear it?'

He had manoeuvred her to one side of a support pillar, his back to the room, discouraging anyone else from joining the conversation.

'It was a gift from a friend. He advised me that something black and strapless would make even *me* look elegant.'

'Some friend.' His sardonic drawl made Nora's eyes light up with militant agreement.

'*Former* friend,' she corrected him with savage relish.

'Personally, I think the shoes were the better buy,' he said.

'The dress was terribly pricy,' she murmured, with a twinge of guilt.

He shrugged. 'So were the outrageously sexy shoes, but they're a work of art in themselves.'

Outrageously sexy? Little thrills ran up and down her spine.

'How do you know what they cost?' As soon as the words were out of her mouth, Nora cursed the foolish naivety of her question. As a wealthy man he was probably used to paying his lovers' bills—and to making sure he got full value for his money!

His wicked smile suggested he had read her mind. 'Because they have a famous Italian name stamped on the sole…and you're still wearing the price tag.' He bent down and laced his fingers around her left ankle, lifting her foot and peeling something off the delicate sole of her shoe. Although she automatically gripped his shoulder for balance, he had acted so swiftly that he had replaced her foot firmly on the ground before she had a chance to wobble. 'I noticed it when we were kneeling down.'

Ignoring the lingering warmth in her tingling ankle, Nora stared at the small adhesive-backed paper square he had pressed on to the back of her hand.

'Oh, my *God*!' she breathed, aghast.

'Don't worry, I don't think anyone would class it as a major social gaffe—' he began in amusement.

'My God, this can't be the *price*!' Nora continued in an outraged whisper. 'This is wrong—it has to be a stock number or something. I can't have paid *that* for a pair of *shoes*! I wouldn't have! It's indecent!'

'Maybe they were on sale,' he murmured, watching her dusting of freckles glow vivid ginger against her blanched skin.

'Expensive hotel boutiques target high-rolling tourists— they don't *have* sales,' she said hollowly. She blinked her thickly mascaraed eyelashes, trying in vain to make the dollar sign in front of the figures go away. 'I don't believe it—they cost almost twice as much as the *dress* did!' She heaved a sigh, screwing up the price sticker until it was a tiny hard pellet and flicking it away.

'How much did you think they cost?' he asked curiously.

'I don't know. I didn't care. I was in such a temper I didn't even look at the price,' she admitted, closing her eyes as she frantically tried to remember what else she had put on her credit card this month.

'A temper?'

'Mmm?' Her eyes flew open and she became enmeshed in his intently curious gaze. Had he noticed that her eyelids were slightly pink and puffy under their lavish powdering of green shadow and gold glitter? She didn't want him to think she was a pathetic weepy female. 'Oh...' She gestured vaguely with her glass and delivered the understatement of all time. 'I was upset about something that happened earlier.'

'And when you're upset, you shop?'

'God, no. I hate shopping...for clothes, anyway.' She shuddered. 'All that standing around, staring at yourself. And I certainly don't get paid enough to buy shoes like this every time I lose my temper!'

'What kind of work do you do?' he asked, propping his arm against the narrow pillar, his wrist skimming the curve of her bare shoulder.

'I help people fix problems with their computers,' she said, deliberately down-playing her skill. She was all too familiar with the glaze that appeared on people's faces when she started talking about her job.

'Here in the city?'

'Our offices are just a few blocks away.' She didn't want to talk about Maitlands. Or even *think* about how she was going to cope with the strain of working in the same office as Ryan—and Kelly—after tonight. 'This is the first time I've been up the Sky Tower, though. Have you been here before?'

'I bring international clients to the restaurant and casino quite regularly. PresCorp has a permanent suite at the hotel. It's also useful for occasions like this, when my workload is so heavy that I don't want to waste time commuting.'

Prickles danced across her skin. 'You're staying here at the hotel?' she blurted huskily. He gave her a speculative look and she fought down a blush. 'Wouldn't a serviced apartment be more cost effective for the company?' she hastened to say.

'Even luxury apartments don't come with twenty-four-hour room service—' He stopped as she suddenly stiffened, the colour draining from her face. 'Is something wrong?'

'No—yes.' She ducked her head below the level of his shoulders, burying her nose in her drink. 'I just realised that I'm famished. I wonder when they're going to serve some proper food.'

'Not for some time yet.' He tilted his wrist so that she could see the face of his steel Rolex. 'Supper at ten-thirty p.m., the invitation said—and there'll be speeches to get through first. Didn't you eat before you came?'

She recalled throwing up in a rainy gutter somewhere, retching her heart out while the tears streamed down her face.

'I wasn't in the mood.'

'There're plenty of nibbles going around. Would you like me to get us some?' He dropped his arm and began to turn.

'No! Don't go!' She clutched at his jacket, her eyes sliding past him.

'I was only going to signal a waiter.' He looked down at her fixed expression, noting the way she had edged around to keep his body between herself and the room, while still keeping whatever was holding her attention in view. 'Someone you didn't expect to see tonight?' he asked shrewdly.

Someone she would be happy never to see again!

With growing outrage, Nora watched Ryan working the room as if he didn't have a care in the world. He had been enormously pleased at the prospect of mixing with some of the city's leading citizens, but he had only received an invitation to the party because he was *her* partner. He certainly knew how to market himself, she'd give him that, but now that the scales had fallen from her eyes she could see him for what he was: a noxious little opportunist!

CHAPTER THREE

'LET me guess...the *former* friend who mistakes fashion for style?' Blake MacLeod murmured, tracking her gaze.

Nora felt a spurt of spiteful amusement as she turned her eyes squarely back to her companion and his impeccably understated elegance.

'His name is Ryan.'

'Is he important?' The supercilious tilt of his eyebrows was a masterly put-down.

Nora smiled brilliantly. 'Not anymore.'

She raised her glass to her lips and was dismayed to see her hand tremble.

It was too much to hope for that the sharp-eyed man she was with wouldn't notice it, too. His eyes flickered down the slender length of her arm and his face turned to stone. 'Are you afraid of him?' he asked quietly.

'Ryan? No, of course not!' she scorned. He had already done his worst and she had survived.

'Did he beat you?'

'Only at squash—I always creamed him at chess and Scrabble!' she replied flippantly.

His expression remained guarded. 'Then how did you get these?' he said, lightly touching his fingertips to the fresh bruises on the inside of her forearm, blotchy shadows blooming through the smooth, translucent skin.

The tiny sizzle that accompanied his touch made her senses scatter. 'What? Oh…I banged my arm against a doorknob at home this afternoon,' she recalled reluctantly. It had been the bathroom door she had been backing out of—her eyes screwed shut against the sight of the guilty pair in the bathtub, scrabbling to separate themselves. The sharp jolt of physical pain in her arm had been a welcome distraction from the agony of her disillusionment as Ryan had followed her, dragging a towel around his hips, blustering in self-defensive anger, turning the blame for his behaviour back on to Nora

'You walked into a door?' Blake said with blunt scepticism. 'Do you realise what a stereotypical answer that is?'

Her eyes widened as she realised that he was seriously concerned that she might be a battered woman. 'But I really did,' she protested. 'I would never let a man get away with being abusive towards me.'

'I thought they looked like fingermarks,' he murmured, aligning his fingers over the blue-brown smudges.

'Well, they're not. I have very sensitive skin. Bruises always show up quickly, looking worse than they are.'

The sight of his lean tanned fingers lying against her skin made her mouth go dry and her body throb with awareness. The contrast between his sinewy brown hand and her delicate paleness seemed starkly erotic. She couldn't believe that a stranger's touch could have such a dramatic impact. On the other hand, she had never before opened herself up to the possibility that another man could arouse her with a mere look, a touch…

She watched as he slowly splayed his hand, gently encircling her arm in a bracelet of warm flesh. She shivered.

'Cold?' he asked, in a knowing voice that said he knew very well what had caused her reaction.

Her eyelids felt heavy, weighted down by lashes as she lifted them to meet his gaze. 'It is rather cool up here.' She uttered the bald-faced lie in the nature of a challenge.

His lips and eyebrows quirked. 'Perhaps the altitude doesn't suit you.'

She wished he hadn't reminded her! 'Or maybe it's the fact that I'm more exposed than usual,' she said, with a hitch of one dappled shoulder.

'Would you like me to put my jacket around you?' he offered.

Nora's hectic emotions translated the private gesture of courtesy into a primitive act of public possession.

'No, you keep it,' she said huskily. 'I wouldn't like you to catch a chill.'

'I don't think there's any fear of that.' His thumb moved on her arm, sliding over the rounded inner curve of her elbow. 'I'm very warm-blooded.'

Her own spurted hotly in her veins. 'That's not what I've heard.'

'And do you always believe everything you're told?' he taunted.

Her pupils contracted to narrow dots, the only sign of her inward flinch. 'I used to.' She couldn't help glancing over to where she had seen Ryan. 'Now I prefer to rely on more tangible evidence.'

Blake's hand left her arm to tilt her head firmly back in his direction, demanding her full attention. 'Very wise. How hungry are you?'

She blinked at his *non sequitur*. 'I beg your pardon?'

'You said you haven't had dinner and, as it happens, neither have I. What say we blow this joint and find a restaurant that can serve us within the next half-hour?'

Blow this joint? His mocking slang made it sound invitingly dangerous, with the added bonus of allowing her to avoid any painful encounters with Ryan.

'But what about the party—?' she stammered, not sure whether he was joking.

'In a crowd this size, one or two less isn't going to matter.'

One or two? Did that mean that he intended leaving, with or without Nora? She felt a stab of disappointment, followed by a fresh surge of reckless determination. When she had singled him out in her sights she had had no idea where her flirtation would lead, or how far she was prepared to take her rash experiment. She still didn't know, but her fear and uncertainty was all part of the intoxicating excitement that jetted through her as she contemplated her next move.

'They might not notice *my* disappearance, but you're a lot higher up the scale of importance,' she felt compelled to point out.

A world of natural arrogance was expressed in his shrug. 'I've done my duty. I came. Waved the PresCorp flag in the necessary faces. Kissed the birthday girl and gave her a gift. More than enough to satisfy Scotty's festering social conscience. Now I'm back on my own time.'

It took her a moment to realise who he meant by 'Scotty'.

'You only came because Sir Prescott Williams asked you to?'

'The word "ask" implies choice. Prescott is far too shrewd to offer options that won't deliver his preferred outcome,' he replied drily. 'He knows exactly how and where to apply pressure. He's an expert in getting his own way.'

'Somehow I can't quite picture you as anyone's helpless pawn. You don't look like a man who enjoys taking orders.'

He threw back the last of his drink and acknowledged her tart remark with an insinuating smile. 'On the contrary, if I perceive a mutual benefit I can be extremely accommodating.'

His soft purr hinted at all sorts of intriguing wickedness. 'Are you saying you'd let *me* order you around?' she said, forbidden images swirling up from the unplumbed depths of her mind.

'Well, not here, obviously—I do have my ruthless image to protect,' he mocked, playing to the shocked curiosity that flared across her face, fascinated by the contradiction between the smouldering passion of those sultry painted eyes and the astringent freshness of her unpredictable personality. It was a long time since Blake had been surprised by anyone or anything. 'Perhaps I'll let you order *for* me in the restaurant, as a start…'

'Restaurant?' In her flurry of wild imaginings she had forgotten the original question.

'You'd rather wait and eat here?' He looked down into his empty glass, masking his expression as he mused, 'Maybe you're right. Even if you're not lucky enough to be assigned a window-seat, once everyone sits down you'll have an uninterrupted view from whichever table you're at, reminding you with every bite that you're in a nine-storey building perched atop a concrete shaft around three hundred metres high but only a bare twelve metres in diameter...'

Nora's stomach did a sickening loop-the-loop, a fine dew springing out on her brow.

'...whereas the restaurant I have in mind is only a quiet ground-floor place around the corner from the casino,' he continued smoothly. 'Good food, but one step down from the street...with absolutely *no* view—'

'Actually, that sounds rather nice,' Nora gulped, clutching gratefully at the dangled safety-line. 'Let's go there.'

Only when the words were out of her mouth did she realise what she had committed herself to, and her stomach performed another crazy loop, this time of excitement. Somehow, she had beguiled one of the city's most cynical bachelors into taking her out to dinner!

He gave her no chance to change her mind. 'Do you need to make any farewells, or do you want to just melt away?'

She should at least exchange a few words with Patty, her former flatmate, and thank her for the invitation. 'Well, I—'

Suddenly, out of the corner of her eye, she saw Ryan and felt a sharp spike of panic.

'Melting would be good,' she said quickly. 'Melting is *very* good—as long as we do it right away.'

If Blake was startled by the rough urgency of her tone he didn't show it. 'Don't you want to finish your drink?' he murmured, half turning to put down his empty glass.

Ryan's face was now a nasty white blot on the periphery of Nora's vision. Had he seen her yet?

Her overwrought imagination bubbled with horrifying scenarios. What if Ryan wanted to appease his guilty conscience with more shattering revelations? What if he decided that by approaching her in public he could compel her to listen to what he had to say?

Ryan knew how much she disliked being the centre of attention—he would be *relying* on it to prevent her from making a scene. He could be doggedly persistent and remarkably ingratiating when it served his own interests. He was even capable, she thought wildly, of following her from the party and turning Blake MacLeod's desirable companion into a dreary woman scorned!

She held out her drink. 'No, thanks, it's gone warm anyway—'

As Blake turned back, a group of chattering people pushed past behind Nora and she was shunted forward. The arm she had extended jerked, the contents of her glass splattering in an arc over Blake's jacket and tie and plastering a fist-sized patch of his shirt to his chest.

There was a stunned pause.

'Oh, God, I'm most terribly sorry!' Nora brushed ineffectually at the splashes on his lapel, which had instantly soaked into the pale sheen of the fabric.

'There's no need to apologise,' he said, taking away her empty glass and handing it to a sympathetic bystander, 'if it wasn't your fault.'

'Those people bumped against me,' she explained, sure her guilt must be written in fire across her forehead.

He looked at her from under his lowered brow. 'So I saw…'

'One of them must have jogged my arm,' she added unnecessarily.

'I suppose I should be grateful that you weren't drinking the Cabernet Sauvignon,' he commented with wry resignation, taking a white linen handkerchief out of his breast pocket and blotting at himself.

If she *had* been drinking red wine she would never have had the courage to do it! she thought, but desperate situations had called for desperate measures. 'I don't think it'll stain if you rinse it out immediately.'

'This suit is made of silk,' he pointed out.

He didn't need to add that it was very expensive Italian-styled silk. Nora had already guessed that it had probably cost more than her top-of-the-line office laptop.

'Oh, dear!' She bit her lip. 'And so is your beautiful tie,' she commiserated. 'If you don't want to risk them being permanently marked you really do need to do something as soon as possible…'

He dabbed at the splotches on his tie. 'What would you suggest?'

Her mouth went dry and she deliberately pitched her voice low to disguise her jittery tension. 'Well…we were leaving anyway, and you said you have a suite at the hotel. Why don't we go there and you can phone the concierge? I'm sure the hotel offers an emergency dry-cleaning service…'

His hand stilled.

'I'm sure they do,' he said, looking into her wide innocent eyes. 'If you're certain you don't mind taking the detour?'

She swallowed, fighting down a blush. 'No, no, not at all. You can't go to the restaurant like that. I'd feel dreadful if you risked ruining your suit because of me.'

It was all she could do not to hustle him along as they began to move across the revolving floor. Unfortunately their progress was slowed by people who sought to waylay Blake, and it was several minutes before they finally made it up the steps to the reception area by the lift bay. In the meantime a furtive glance over her shoulder showed her Ryan's startled face, mooning at her from the crowd as he set out on an intersecting course.

Nora stalked towards the glass doors, only to find herself stayed by Blake's polite command.

'If you wait here, I'll collect your coat and umbrella.'

'Oh, but—' She found herself talking to empty air. She

would gladly have abandoned the wretched things for the sake of a quick getaway. Stranded on elevated ground, she had no place to hide when the unwelcome voice sounded behind her.

'Nora? Nora—I know you saw me. I can't believe you're here! Thank goodness you're all right!'

She turned reluctantly, plastering a look of surprise on her face. '*I* was invited, remember? Why shouldn't I be here? Why are *you*?'

Ryan mounted the last step, his even features bearing a tentative conciliating smile. 'Well, we'd accepted the invitation. I thought at least one of us should come, and I didn't think that you'd make it all the way up here by yourself. You were so upset when you took off from the flat, I didn't know what to think! We were worried about you....'

He dared mention Kelly? As if either of them had cared a fig about her feelings when they were wallowing in her bath!

She stared haughtily down at him, unimpressed by his attempt to smooth things over. She had always seen him as a lovable, cuddly teddy bear—with his curly blond hair, button-bright blue eyes, square jaw and stocky physique. Now she could see his brash charm was a threadbare illusion, the careless affection with which he had captured her dreams no substitute for genuine passion.

'Well, you needn't have—as you can see, I'm fine,' she said abruptly. He must have remembered the system profiles that she had been creating for his current project, beavering away in her spare time for weeks so that Ryan could gain extra kudos from his boss—who also happened to be Kelly's uncle!

His eyes were puzzled as they travelled over her, trying to work out what was different—so different—about her. Finally it clicked and he looked down.

'My God, Nora, where on earth did you get those *ridiculous* shoes? You'll likely break your neck in them. Besides, they make you look like a beanpole.'

A few hours ago she might have meekly agreed with him, but Nora's blood was up.

'Look, Ryan, I'd love to stand around and chat all night,' she said with heavy sarcasm, 'but as it happens I have better things to do.'

His patronising confidence said he didn't believe her. What could be more important to Nora than the man she had been mooning over since she was twenty?

'Give me a break, Nora,' he appealed, producing the whee-dling little-lost-boy smile that she used to think was adorable. 'We need to talk. You didn't give me time to explain what I meant this afternoon. I never wanted to hurt you, you know, Nora—'

'Then you shouldn't have slept with my flatmate!' she said icily.

'We all make mistakes, Nora. We've known each other for years. I'd still like us to be friends, especially since we work at the same place—'

Of course he would, because then he could continue to tap into her specialised talent to enhance his own career. When he had been at university and she had been working in the technology lab, he had noticed her unrequited crush and persuaded her to give him free tutoring to help him pass his computer and statistics papers. As well as helping him out with research she had also typed up his assignments and edited the bad grammar and fuzzy logic out of his essays, all for the sake of a few platonic hugs and kisses and the privilege of being accepted into his magic circle of friends. And five years later she was still helping him to make a good impression at the expense of her own needs.

'I've decided it's time I graduated to a better class of friend.'

He laid a heavy hand on her wrist. 'Come on, Eleanor, you don't mean that,' he said thinly. 'Everyone makes mistakes.'

'Yes, and you were mine,' she said, clinging to her self-control.

His hand tightened. 'If it wasn't for me you'd still be stuck in some dreary little cubicle somewhere—'

'Ready to go, Nora?' The deep voice resonated in her bones and with a start she realised that Blake MacLeod was standing behind her, holding out her open coat. Instead of feeling embarrassed at what he might have overheard, Nora was emboldened by his solid strength at her back.

Ryan's hand fell from her arm, his jaw going slack as he focused on the man taking her bag while he helped her into her coat. 'You're leaving with *him*?'

'I told you I had better things to do.' It gave her a malicious pleasure to say.

He didn't appear to hear her, hastily extending his hand to take advantage of the unexpected encounter. 'Uh, Mr MacLeod, we haven't met, but of course I know who you are—I'm Ryan Trent—'

To Nora's delight Blake ignored the eagerly outstretched hand, returning her bag and hooking her umbrella over his arm so that he could adjust the collar of her coat, his knuckles brushing with gentle deliberation along the tense line of her jaw.

'I have in mind something far more succulent for you to sink your teeth into,' he told her with shameless eroticism, pressing his thumb against the swollen lower lip she had been unconsciously abusing. 'I hope you're still as hungry as I am…'

'More,' she said throatily, falling in with his baiting game, her teeth briefly grating against his salty thumb which he withdrew to place between his lips.

Tasting her. His tongue flicked out, a provocative dart that only she could see, and suddenly it was no longer a game.

'Shall we?' he murmured, placing his flat hand low on her back, and Nora went warm all over, steaming up the inside of her coat.

'Eleanor!' Ryan's shocked voice held the hint of an aggrieved whine as she began to move. 'I thought we were going to talk—'

'Some other time, Ryan,' she tossed out carelessly. 'And, oh!' She paused beside him, savouring the advantage of her dominating height. 'I never noticed it before, Ryan, but maybe you should see someone about that thinning patch on the top of your head—it's a classic sign of premature male-pattern baldness….'

She sashayed on by, leaving Ryan, his hand smoothing

uneasily over his crown, staring after them, his face a blotchy rash of angry colour.

'Beautiful,' said Blake in admiration as they sauntered out through the glass door, and Nora knew he wasn't talking about her. 'Is he really going bald?' he asked as he summoned the lift.

'If there's any justice in the world. Ryan's very vain about his hair. He'll drive himself crazy worrying about it.'

'Probably feel insecure about it for the rest of his life.' The shiny metal doors hissed open and he indicated with the umbrella for her to precede him. 'You're clearly a dangerous woman to cross.'

She liked the sound of that. Even the hint of laughter in his voice couldn't dent her triumphant confidence as she stepped over the threshold. 'Yes, I am.'

'In that case I'll be careful to stay on your good side,' he said, following her in. 'Which is it, left or right?'

The wet patch on his shirt was low over his heart, the white cotton sticking transparently to his olive skin, showing the fine tangle of black hair on his chest. She thought she could also see his bronzed nipple, but she wasn't sure whether it was just a shadow of a curl.

'Nora?'

'Hmm?' Her coat rustled as she started guiltily, gesturing towards his open jacket. 'I'm awfully sorry about what happened with the wine,' she said, barely registering the sound of the door sliding shut, enclosing them in a hush of privacy.

He shrugged, dragging the dampened shirt taut across his skin. 'I'm not; it saved me from a slow drowning in a sea of social platitudes.' Definitely a nipple, thought Nora dizzily, feeling like a sleazy voyeur for noticing.

'Since it's still raining outside, and we're going to the suite anyway, perhaps you'd prefer to relax there and order dinner from the room service menu,' he continued, pressing the button for the ground floor and turning to face her.

Nora's breathing quickened under his quizzical gaze. They both knew there was nothing innocent about his casual offer.

It had not escaped him that she had virtually invited herself to his room, and now he was politely testing the waters, asking her to clarify her expectations in terms that a virtuous young lady was safe to misinterpret.

He was letting her know that all she had to do was refuse and the rest of the evening would be conducted under the conventional rules of propriety—a pleasant meal in a public restaurant, a light flirtation…final outcome: uncertain.

But Nora wasn't feeling virtuous or conventional. She knew that there was no respectable excuse for her to accept his loaded offer; she had already successfully evaded Ryan and salved some of her deeply wounded pride. But that 'beanpole' taunt still rankled, and no man had never looked at her in the way that Blake was looking at her now—with a blatant sexual speculation that ate her up with curiosity.

Her stomach flip-flopped as the lift began its rapid descent. She was conscious that he was watching and waiting as she hovered on the brink of the precipice. She hastily turned away, hugging her evening bag to her pounding breast with both hands.

'I think that sounds—' The words froze on her tongue as she found herself staring straight out through the rain-smeared glass front of the lift. Everything tilted, her blood roaring in her ears, a metallic taste flooding her mouth, her body going rigid, limbs paralysed with shock. The lights of the city blurred into coloured streamers that lashed back and forth, reaching through the glass, trying to pull her headlong into that rushing void, binding her chest until she was unable to breathe, to think, to save herself from falling, falling…

'Nora?' Blake's sharp voice pierced her consciousness but, encased in an icy block of fear, she was helpless to frame a coherent response, an indistinct mewing sound issuing from her bloodless lips, her fingernails bending as they dug into her bag.

She heard him swear fluently, cursing his own thoughtlessness. A protective arm whipped around her waist, turning her aside from the cold glass, drawing her against the reassuring warmth of human flesh.

'Don't look.'

He didn't understand, she thought, screwing her head sideways in order to keep the mesmerising horror in sight. She couldn't *not* look. Imagination was far worse than terrifying reality.

'Nora, it's all right, you're safe with me—you've only got to hold on for a little while longer. Close your eyes, if it helps….'

And let the nightmare of falling completely take over? She shook her head violently, a silent scream building up in her throat.

He cursed again and she dimly heard a rattling thud as he dropped her furled umbrella. 'Nora, stop looking down—' He grasped her jaw in his hand, far more roughly than he had at the party, and forced her eyes to meet his compelling gaze. 'Don't worry about what's out there…look at *me*.'

Her head jerked in mindless panic. 'I can't—'

Instead of impatiently snapping at her to pull herself together, as Ryan had done whenever she had revealed her weakness, he firmed his grip, his voice quiet, slow and forceful. 'Yes, you can. Focus on me. Concentrate. Breathe deeply and think of something else, something you want more than *anything*—'

'Like what?' she choked despairingly, her slender body beginning to ripple with chills, the blood draining from her extremities to warm her icy core.

His eyes fell to her mouth and blazed with a fierce determination. 'Like this…'

He bent his head, blotting out the world, his mouth crushing down on her cold lips, sealing in her ragged breath, invading her with his masculine heat and iron will sheathed in a wet velvet tongue. The arm around her waist slid down and tightened, arching her hips against the centre of his body, his other hand flattening between her shoulderblades, his palm hot against her bare skin as he locked her to his chest, trapping her folded arms between their bodies, leaving her helpless to resist his devouring hunger. The assault was sudden and brutal, an erotic smash-and-grab raid which swamped her fear in a flood of pleasure, robbing her of everything but the desperate need to feel him thrust harder, hotter, deeper inside her...

He cupped her head, changing the angle of his kiss to allow him deeper access, smothering her with his scent, his taste, sucking at her lower lip, scraping at her with his teeth, luring her tongue into a seductive battle inside his mouth, battering her with violently delightful sensations.

She squirmed to get closer, her chills turned to a raging fever, burning away her inhibitions, her awareness of time and place. She groaned as she felt him subtly pull back from the kiss, but it was only to allow her to free her arms. Her evening bag plopped unnoticed on top of her umbrella as her hands slid eagerly up under the back of his jacket, fingers clawing at the soft cotton of his shirt, her short-trimmed nails biting into his hot skin through the thin fabric.

His muscles tensed and he growled a warning deep in his throat, the sound of a hungry male predator staking claim over his captive prey. A new, entirely delicious fear feathered along Nora's nerves and she flexed her nails again, revelling in his lightning-swift response to the feline goad. She gasped, the sound lost in his plundering mouth as he unleashed another burst of aggressive passion, prowling her backwards until her shoulders hit the padded corner of the lift, caging her there with his lean, hard body while he greedily satisfied her feminine curiosity. His hands slid to her waist, anchoring her to the wall, then sliding up to splay over the slight curve of her breasts, his fingertips curling into the top edge of her dress as if he would wrench it down, his hard knee pushing between her legs, his strong, sinewy thigh jamming itself intimately against the melting centre of her body.

'Uh, excuse me...,'

A polite cough had Blake wrenching his mouth from hers and for a few thundering heartbeats he stared at her, his breathing uneven, his grey eyes slightly stunned, his expression tight.

'Excuse me, Mr MacLeod, but I need to let the lift go. Were you intending to get off here—or um…?'

Blake spun around and Nora flushed to the roots of her hair as she straightened and met the brightly curious stare of the liveried young man who was politely restraining the twitch of the automatic doors.

She hadn't even been aware of the lift coming to a halt, let alone the doors opening. The whole journey had probably taken less than thirty seconds but she felt as if she had acquired the experience of a lifetime!

CHAPTER FOUR

To HIDE her blushing confusion Nora ducked to pick up her umbrella and freshly abused evening bag, sending up a silent prayer of thanks that it hadn't broken its makeshift wire catch. When she looked up again it was to see Blake tucking something into the young man's breast pocket, murmuring a low-voiced remark into his reddened ear before turning back to place a guiding hand under Nora's elbow.

'What were you saying to him?' she asked breathlessly, her heels wobbling to keep pace with his long impatient strides.

'I merely reminded him that as a regular visitor I know I can rely on his discretion,' he said, leading her on to the escalator that would take them up to the main entrance to the casino complex.

'You were paying him to keep his mouth shut,' she guessed, not sure whether to be admiring or disapproving.

'Merely a small token of my appreciation,' he demurred. 'I also suggested that he share his bounty with the person who monitors the security cameras.'

'Th-There was a camera in the lift?' she stammered, blushing anew as she imagined her passionate frenzy splashed across a flickering screen somewhere in the bowels of the building. 'I hope we don't turn up on some "caught on video" reality programme,' she muttered shakily.

'I don't think they'd be interested in anything so tame.'

'*Tame?*' Nora stared at him wide-eyed, her fingers tightening nervously on the moving hand-rail.

'We kept our clothes on,' he pointed out as they reached the top of the escalator.

'Oh, yes, of course...' she muttered, slightly reassured.

'Although I must admit it was touch and go there for a moment,' he added slyly, and Nora gave a little yelp as she mistimed her step off the moving pad, hooking her heel on the metal rim and lurching drunkenly against him.

'I'm sorry,' she said, ultra-conscious of the coiled tension in his flexing muscles. 'I—I guess I'm still feeling a bit weak at the knees—'

He didn't even break stride, his hand sliding from her elbow to her wrist, supporting the full weight of her stumble with his braced forearm. 'I'm flattered.'

His confident amusement ruffled her pride. 'I was talking about the lift!'

'So was I,' he drawled, negotiating what seemed like a maze of pillars and walkways at a pace which had Nora's loose coat billowing out behind her and rendered her even more breathless and light-headed. Blake MacLeod was clearly a very goal-orientated man, as decisive in his actions as he was in his ideas. Swept up in his whirlwind energy, Nora wondered darkly whether any woman had ever succeeded in making *him* weak at the knees.

He slowed down slightly, only because they had reached the plush hotel foyer and were approaching a bank of lifts. The door to one of the lifts instantly hummed open, as if to his silent decree.

'Open sesame!' Nora murmured, contemplating the empty, elegantly lit interior with a *frisson* of alarm.

'How fortunate for both of us that you know the secret password.' Blake distracted her with his sensuous purr, using his body to shepherd her gently over the threshold.

It was on the tip of her tongue to tell him that cracking passwords was one of her professional specialities, but that would be far too prosaic. 'I thought everyone did,' she said huskily.

'Only those conversant with *The Arabian Nights*. And knowing what words to say is useless unless you know where and when to say them. You enjoy romantic tales of the imagination?' he asked, moving over to the control panel.

'It beats reality any day,' she said with a wry twist of her mouth.

'Maybe your previous reality just hasn't been exciting enough to compete with your imaginative desires.' His deep lazy tone was an implicit promise to remedy the fact.

Her 'previous reality' had complained about her *lack* of imagination, but her disturbingly intense response to Blake's caressing words and flagrant handling put an entirely different slant on Ryan's taunts about Nora's sexual shortcomings. Now she wondered if it hadn't been her awareness of his impatience and an over-anxious desire to please which had inhibited her lovemaking. She wouldn't have to worry about pleasing Blake MacLeod in bed. She had complete confidence that he would please himself no matter what she did or didn't do!

She moistened her dry lips and his eyes narrowed on her tense face. 'If this is really a problem for you, we could take the stairs,' he said, flattening his hand across both door controls to prevent the lift from moving.

She was stunned by his thoughtfulness. 'N-no, I'm fine. I'm OK as long as I can't see where we are on the vertical scale…' An awful thought struck her. 'You aren't in the penthouse suite, are you?'

His head moved fractionally in the negative, his grey eyes absorbing her relief as she sighed. 'You must think I'm a terrible coward…'

'Must I?' His raised eyebrows expressed surprise that anybody should tell him what to think.

She lifted her chin. 'I know it seems irrational—'

'Feelings frequently are illogical—it doesn't make them any less valid.' He shrugged. 'Our primitive instincts and basic drives often cause havoc with our rational selves…we call it being human.'

She was wary of his understanding. 'I hope you don't think I'm weak and over-emotional just because I'm a woman.'

'God forbid,' he said drily, finally setting the lift in motion with a casual tap of a knuckle. 'Some of the strongest and most ruthlessly unsentimental people I know are women.' He leaned back against the wall of the lift and folded his arms across his chest, regarding her flushed face with a smoky satisfaction. 'And as a man I'm quite happy to admit that there are times when allowing one's primitive urges free rein is deeply rewarding….'

When he suddenly chuckled it was a stinging reminder of another man's belittlement.

Her eyes blazed at him. 'What's so funny?'

'I was just thinking…you'd make a good model for Boadicea right now—tall and queenly, feminine and fierce, draped in a flowing raiment and carrying your bag and umbrella clasped to your bosom like a sword and shield.'

To Nora's chagrin she realised that she was indeed clutching her accessories in front of her like defensive weapons. She forced herself to nonchalantly lower her arms.

'If I'm Boadicea who are you…one of my lowly English serfs?'

His eyes gleamed with appreciation. 'I rather saw myself as a Roman general accepting your surrender.'

Nora tossed her autumn-brown head in unconscious challenge. No man was ever again going to bemoan her passiveness. 'I don't think Boadicea ever surrendered herself to the Romans, did she?'

'Actually, I think she chose to take poison rather than bow her head in defeat,' he said, pushing himself off the wall as the lift pinged its arrival at the selected floor. 'You look as if you admire her courage. Is my captive warrior queen getting cold feet?' he murmured against the rumble of the opening door. The words were playful, but the underlying message was not.

Colour streaked across Nora's cheeks. 'I'm nobody's captive!'

'Very impressive, but that doesn't answer my question.'

She looked him straight in the eye, concealing her angry turmoil, determined to be bold and assertive.

'You're the one who seems to be having second thoughts, *General*. Afraid you can't handle me without a legion at your back?'

Silver light flared in his storm-dark eyes and hot blood pulsed through the vein in his exposed temple.

'I already have,' he reminded her with a lethal smile steeped in male arrogance. He braced his hand across the gap into which the sliding door had retracted. 'And, as I recall, you would have been on your knees if I hadn't been holding you up.'

'I thought that was where you wanted me to be,' she shot back.

'Oh, it is...but I'd prefer to wait until we're both naked.' He was swift to take advantage of her unwitting *double-entendre*. 'It's much more satisfying that way.'

She blushed from head to foot but valiantly battled on. 'Maybe *you'll* be the one brought to your knees.'

His eyelids lowered over his sultry amusement. 'I'd like that. I'm all for equal opportunity in the bedroom.'

Her mouth went dry as she thought of this aggressive and strong-willed male submitting himself to her every whim, his sleek, muscled body her erotic playground, his sexual expertise hers to command. 'And out of it?'

'I like to think of myself as a fair man. Is it relevant?'

Of course it wasn't. She was just wasting time. She swallowed hard, trying to work some moisture into her mouth so her voice wouldn't come out as a nervous croak. 'Which way is your suite?'

'To the right—the *right*,' he repeated, hooking her by the elbow as she veered in the wrong direction.

'Sorry,' she muttered, flustered by her mistake. 'I'm left-handed.'

'That explains everything,' he said, with a dry humour which made her feel a shade less foolish.

'Well, I'm right-brained, but ambidextrous when it comes to doing most things,' she expanded. 'That's why I get mixed up sometimes.'

He came to a halt in front of a panelled door and swiped the keycard across the lock, standing aside to usher her inside, flicking a switch to softly illuminate the long room. On their lowest setting, the lamps cast a mellow glow over the whipped cream carpet, plush sofas and art-strung walls. To Nora's surprised relief, Blake's next action was to cross to the full-length windows and draw the heavy curtains across what was undoubtedly a superb view of the city.

A little of her tension eased and she placed her umbrella and bag down on the narrow entrance table, moving further into the luxurious cocoon. There was a desk stacked with papers and files and an ultra-slim laptop computer blinking in sleep-mode; next to it a sideboard held a television and video game machine, coffee-making facilities and a heavily stocked mini-bar. A mahogany table with six ladder-backed chairs was angled to take advantage of the view. A large basket of fresh flowers and tropical fruits graced the coffee table between the cushioned sofas, and through the archway to her left the spill of light along the floor showed Nora a wedge of bathroom floor and, beyond that, the edge of a king-sized bed receding into the darkness, the turned-down sheet and plumped pillows at its head shimmering ghostly white in the gloom.

'I don't think it's likely to rain in here, do you?'

'I beg your pardon?' She tore her eyes hurriedly away from the beckoning fantasy to find Blake prowling back in her direction.

'Your coat. Would you like to take it off?'

'Oh…yes…' Anxious not to seem gauche, she hastily peeled the lapels, her fingers all thumbs, until he stepped around behind her, stilling her jerky movements with a light touch on her shoulders.

'Allow me.' Unlike Nora, he was in no hurry. His warm palms cupped her supple shoulders as he eased the sleeves free and slid them slowly down her arms, his fingertips trickling down her bare skin in their wake, caressing her from the tender crease in her armpits to her delicate inner wrists.

'Thank you,' she murmured, standing stiffly straight as he tossed the coat carelessly across the corner of the desk, his hands returning to bracelet her dangling wrists, trapping them at her sides. He bent his head, his silky black hair brushing her cheek as he rested his mouth against the smooth dip of her shoulder.

'My pleasure,' he said, his breath fanning over her skin, his lips stroking her as they shaped the words, making her wish he was more loquacious. Her head tilted to grant him greater access and he made a low sound of approval, shifting his mouth closer to the curve of her throat.

'There's something slightly barbaric about a woman showing this much bare skin without the civilising distraction of jewellery.' He feathered his lips along the ridge of her collarbone. 'Is that why you decided not to wear anything around your throat? Because you knew how temptingly naked it would make you look?'

Nora's hands involuntarily clenched at the gentle rake of his teeth, a shocking pang of sweetness spearing through her body. The thought of herself as a brazen temptress was wildly arousing but she didn't think she could sustain the role of calculating vamp, not when a simple touch of his mouth rendered her a jumble of confused longings. The exhilarating sense of danger was now even more acute, his stance shifting, his hips crowding her slim bottom, leaving her in no doubt as to the intensity of his interest. 'I—I left home in a rush,' she admitted thickly. 'I just didn't happen to have time to think about jewellery.'

'Then it's up to me to provide you with suitable adornment,' he murmured, nuzzling aside a veil of curls to string a necklace of slow kisses over her vulnerable nape, placing each one as carefully as if it was a precious jewel. The sharp rasp of his hair-roughened chin was a spine-tingling contrast to the velvet softness of his lips, and with each successive kiss her nerves tightened another notch. His hands moved down to enclose her balled fists, making her excitingly aware of his potentially crushing strength, his mouth ranging back out to the smooth roundness of her shoulder. 'Mmm, I've always wondered how freckles would taste…you have a very interesting cluster right here…' She felt the hot, wet stab of his tongue.

'I—I have freckles everywhere,' she pointed out shakily. No doubt his interchangeably gorgeous women were all creamy-skinned natural beauties, or sported carefully applied tans, and never had to worry about spots or blemishes on their polished complexions—certainly nothing so unsophisticated as a common freckle!

'*Everywhere?*' he teased huskily. She felt his teeth, followed by a moist suction against her skin. 'Is that my invitation to a private tasting?'

The image he evoked made her shiver, her eyes closing, her head falling back against his shoulder. She didn't care if she appeared to be surrendering too easily to his seductive technique. She had incited this, so she was the one who was controlling events. She felt gloriously empowered by his obvious arousal. She wanted—*needed*—to immerse herself in the dazzling sensations that were rolling over her, to prove that she was a woman of passion, worthy of a man's desiring. She wanted to have her womanhood reaffirmed in the most raw and elemental way. And not just by any man, but by this one—a connoisseur of women, a practised warrior in the eternal battle of the sexes, who could show her all she had been missing by clinging to a rosy delusion of love with a man who didn't want her—who had *never* really wanted her….

His hands tightened over hers in silent acknowledgement of her acquiescence, then flattened out against her thighs, smoothing slowly up over the front of her dress, her flat stomach, her trembling ribs, to come to rest just beneath her taut breasts.

To her shock he stepped abruptly away and she heard a slither of sound. Stricken with frustrated disappointment, she turned and saw that he had stripped off his jacket and was wrenching his loosened tie from his collar, flicking open the buttons of his shirt with his other hand, revealing a wedge of tawny chest dusted with blue-black hair and a belly that rippled with lean muscle as he twisted to free his shirt-tails from his belt. She could only stand and stare, her temperature shooting sky-high, while he shrugged free of the shirt, his tanned arms bulging with latent strength. If he had seemed formidably masculine to her before, bare-chested he looked like the very essence of male virility.

His expression was a dark mask of lustful intent, the skin drawn tight across his bones emphasising the intimidating harshness of his face. His eyes burned in their deep sockets, the coal-black shadow on his pugnacious jaw making him look uncompromisingly tough, his slashing widow's peak adding a faintly satanic air to his smouldering regard. He looked primed and ready to take her, body and soul.

Nora took an uncertain step back. His nostrils flared as if he scented her sudden doubt, and then he was reaching for her, gathering her up and driving her back until her legs bumped against the side of the desk. In the same forceful motion his mouth was swooping down on hers, drinking in her shocked gasp as she threw up her hands and they came into contact with the hot skin of his chest, her fingers automatically curling into the soft thicket of dark hair, hanging on for dear life as he deepened his plundering kiss. He tasted of wine—a rich, earthy, complex blend of flavours exploding on her tongue, an intoxicating vintage better than any *premier cru*. Nora melted into the ravishing assault, her senses reeling, her body swept into a tumultuous current that bore her violently away from the shores of logical thought.

His hands went under her arching back and she suddenly felt her zip parting all the way down to the base of her spine. She wrenched her mouth from his, instinctively grabbing at the loosened dress as it fell away, but her scrabbling fingers tangled with deft masculine hands that had other ideas.

'It's all right, this time there's no one here to see you but me…' he murmured, pushing the bunched dress down to her slender hips as her oxygen-starved lungs struggled for breath.

He looked down at the sheer stretchy bandeau bra covering her heaving breasts and his mouth tilted up.

'You don't really need to wear this at all, do you?' he said, toying with the lace-trimmed edge of the narrow black band.

She stiffened defensively, arching back against the arm around her waist, but then his finger dipped to delicately trace the outline of a rigid nipple where it had eagerly flattened itself against the transparent mesh. Splinters of painful pleasure prickled through her swollen flesh as he continued in a tone of honeyed admiration, 'They're as tantalising as ripe apples, so pretty and round and firm that you don't need any artificial support….' His fingers moved to the adjacent peak, chafing it lightly through the thin fabric as his other hand skilfully flicked open the plastic catch at her back. There was no clumsy fumbling, nothing to disrupt the erotic spell he was weaving with his hands and mouth and voice.

'See,' he whispered as her bra followed the path of her dress and her creamy tip-tilted breasts swayed and settled high against her slender ribcage. It was all done so smoothly that Nora didn't have time to feel shy, although her breasts grew rosy under his caressing gaze. 'Firm and round and speckled with warm little freckles.' He drew her briefly against his naked chest, rubbing her dusky pink nipples back and forth against his skin, his hands cupping her shoulderblades. 'Now, let's see if they taste as sweet as they look and feel….'

He bent his head and sipped at the swollen tips, lapping at her with a delicate greed that made her head swim. She couldn't believe she had come so far so fast. Instead of the long, slow build-up she was used to, everything was happening with breakneck speed. With a little moan Nora sank her hand into his thick black hair, the silky strands sifting through her fingers as they clenched in convulsive pleasure. The bevelled edge of the desk, lightly padded by the folds of her discarded coat, cut into her bottom and trapped her crumpled dress around her hips as he tipped her back, attempting to rid them of the annoying impediment to greater intimacy. Squirming to help, Nora gasped as her elbow knocked against a neat stack of files, sending them spilling across the desk and floor.

He stifled the apology that automatically rose to her lips with a fiercely impatient kiss, sweeping her off her feet and stepping over the scattered mess to perch her on the padded arm of the nearby sofa, her dress still twisted around her legs. Nora clung to his satin-smooth shoulders, her mouth eagerly responding to his fiery demands, her heart knocking as she felt his left hand touch her knee beneath the folds of her dress. His teeth tugged at her lower lip, his hand sleeking up the inside of her thigh, finding the elastic top of her stocking and exploring the petal-soft skin just above it. Liquid heat exploded in her belly and she tried to clench her legs together to ease the ache he was creating, but his heavy thigh intruded, forcing them further apart.

Nora could feel the tension quivering in his whipcord muscles, the carnal hunger crouching for the kill. His body exuded a musky male scent that drugged her senses, her hands slipping on the sheen of sweat which coated his tawny skin. She dimly realised that she was no longer in control, if she ever had been.

'Wait—' she panted, jerking violently as she felt the brush of his fingers against the thin fabric which hid the creamy heart of her desire, almost fainting at the gush of pleasure released by the brief contact.

'I can't—' His prickly jaw rasped across her skin, creating a stinging trail of sweet pain as he ate his way down to her throbbing nipple. He suckled hotly, pushing up his knee until she was astride his leg. 'I need this too much…and so do you,' he growled roughly. She felt his arm tighten around her waist, dragging her weight down against his contracting muscles, setting up a friction that turned the delicious pressure between her legs into an electrifying thrill. 'Come on, baby—ride me,' he invited hoarsely, rocking her against his powerful thigh until she adopted his urgent rhythm. Her breathing quickened, her fingers digging into his naked chest, her eyes glazing over as her body responded recklessly to his primal urging. He threw his head back, his glittering eyes darkly triumphant as she began to ripple with tiny convulsions.

'That's right, baby, ride me all the way home…. Let me make it happen for you…' he coaxed huskily, his knowing fingers finding again that secret sweet spot, tracing the blossoming dampness of her bikini panties in a way that made something inside her ripen and burst. Her world shattered into a million pieces, an exquisite avalanche of pleasure cascading through her, carrying her over the brink of a sweeping precipice and flinging her far out into star-studded space. Suddenly she was in a floating free fall…spiralling into nothingness, and yet there was no fear, just a soaring sense of release, the wondrous freedom of realising that she could fly…!

When her eyes fluttered back into focus the fractured world had re-formed around her, forever changed. She was conscious of the damp bloom of her skin and the small aftershocks which rolled over her as she eased back against Blake's locked arms and met his hooded gaze. She could feel the coiled tension in his muscles and felt mortified as she realised what had happened.

She bit her lip and winced at its swollen sensitivity. 'I'm—'

'I hope you're not going to say you're sorry,' he interrupted her with a growl.

'But I—you—' Her freckled face was so enchantingly dismayed that his rigid jaw flickered with sultry amusement.

'I said I couldn't wait. I wanted you wild for me,' he said in a voice like smooth dark chocolate. 'I got what I wanted.'

'I—you did?' Her golden eyes were still muddied with doubt.

'It was incredibly sexy seeing you lose control,' he said,

flexing his hips between hers, letting her feel the iron-hard proof of his words. 'Wanna play turnabout?'

Not exactly sure what he was suggesting, Nora nervously licked her lips and he uttered a sharp groan. 'I take it that's a yes,' he said, divesting her of the trailing dress with a few quick tugs and sinking into a crouch to slide her daring shoes off her unresisting feet. On the way back up he trailed his fingers over the front of her stockings and plain white panties, while he pressed kisses into her dappled skin. But as he rose between her breasts he froze, a frown thundering across his brow.

'My God, what's this?' He touched the crimson abrasions on the side of her breast, recoiling as she winced.

'It's nothing…I told you before, I have very sensitive skin,' she said dismissively.

He swore under his breath, his eyes following the tell-tale path of reddened patches. 'Damn it, stop trying to take the blame for something that's entirely my fault!' He dragged his hand across the coarse black stubble on his chin. 'I haven't shaved since this morning; no wonder I almost rubbed you raw,' he castigated himself.

He sounded so horrified that she almost smiled. 'But you didn't. Really, it's all right.'

'No, it's not,' he said grimly. 'I hurt you. I wasn't thinking—' He gently stroked her reddened breast and she trembled.

'Neither was I,' she tried to convince him. 'How could I have—uh—*you know*…if I thought what you were doing was painful?'

His eyes flamed. 'I'm likely to be a great deal less restrained in the throes of an orgasm,' he said bluntly, disdaining her feeble euphemism. 'I'm bigger and stronger than you are. I don't want to risk hurting you like that when I'm inside you—I'm going to have a shave before I touch you again,' he said, stepping back from temptation.

Nora immediately felt self-conscious, wrapping her empty arms around her semi-nude body to disguise her lack of curves. With a smouldering look at her innocently provocative pose, Blake bent and picked up his shirt, dropping it loosely around her shoulders from whence it hung almost to her knees, scooping her hair out from under the collar and fluffing it out around her oval face.

'Better?' he commented, drawing the open sides across her breasts where they peeked at him from her sheltering arms, not hiding the fact that he found her unexpected shyness arousing.

'Hadn't you better pick up your jacket, too?' she said jerkily. 'You're supposed to be arranging for your suit to be cleaned—'

'I thought that was just an excuse for you to get my clothes off,' he murmured, and she lowered her eyes guiltily.

'It's still going to need professional treatment.'

'Especially since we seem to be adding a new category of stain,' he goaded, drawing her attention to the damp spot on his trousers where she had straddled his thigh.

Nora blushed at the graphic evidence of her violent excitement, her flustered reaction turning his mockery into smouldering concupiscence.

'Maybe I should have that shave before this conversation goes any further,' he said, dropping a quick hard kiss on to her parted lips. 'Feel free to help yourself from the mini-bar; anything I have is yours...'

And with all my worldly goods I thee endow? Nora flinched at the interpretation that popped into her head. She knew he was talking about a glass of wine and a bag of nuts, not a lifetime of loving trust and mutual sharing.

Nora snaked her arms into the sleeves of his shirt as he headed for the bathroom, her eyes falling on the shambles they had made of the desk. In her confused emotional state it suddenly seemed vitally important to restore a sense of order to her physical surroundings. Perhaps that way she might bring some order to her chaotic feelings, find her way back to that liberating sense of *rightness* that she had felt whilst in his arms.

'What are you doing?'

She turned, papers slipping from her nerveless hand, her

eyes widening at his altered appearance. He wore a plush white three-quarter length towelling robe with the hotel's monogram discreetly embroidered on the breast pocket. He was frowning, but more in impatience than suspicion, and she waved one hand helplessly in the air.

'Just tidying up—trying to make myself useful...'

'Forget it,' he ordered dismissively. 'I didn't bring you here to play the domestic.' He caught her fluttering hand and tugged her towards him, lifting her palm to his still scratchy chin. 'I've decided I need a shower as well as a shave. I came to the party straight from work, in the same clothes I've been wearing all day.'

He lowered her hand to the burnished wedge of chest revealed by his loosely tied bathrobe, holding it there as he walked slowly backwards, drawing her along after him. 'If you have a compulsion for neatness, I'm sure you prefer your lovers to be freshly laundered...'

Nora could feel the heavy beat of his heart reverberating through flesh and bone. 'You don't have to bother on my account,' she said breathlessly, obliquely informing him that she liked his earthy male aroma.

He tipped his head to one side, his mellow voice caressing. 'For *my* sake, then.'

His eyes ran over her pale limbs, glimmering at him through the gaps in his shirt. 'I rather thought I might entice you to join me. You can make yourself useful as my soap bearer....'

He had reached the door of the steamy bathroom, the sound of the pulsing shower-head within almost drowned out by the thunder of blood in Nora's ears.

'Perhaps while I'm shaving you might like to wash my back—and anything else that takes your fancy...' he drawled.

He must know that she found *everything* about him wildly fanciable! The provocative admission trembled on the tip of her tongue, until she glanced past him and saw the gleaming empty bath next to the heat-misted glass shower cabinet.

In her mind's eye the bath expanded to take up the whole

room, her memory filling it with a kaleidoscope of flickering images that made her desire curdle in her stomach.

Nightmare reality crashed into her fantasy-fuelled dream world.

What on earth was she *doing*?

She fell back, slipping her hand out of his, flattening it defensively over her heart.

His eyebrows rose. 'No?' Clearly, rejection was a rather startling novelty.

'I—I think...I'd rather not, if you don't mind,' she managed lightly, edging further out of sight of the bath and the spectral frolics that had visited her with a degrading sense of *déjà vu*.

She braced herself for a backlash of wounded male pride, but Blake's grey eyes were merely quizzical.

'Don't tell me that you have a phobia about water, too?' he said.

Nora shook her head dumbly, tucking a curl behind her ear with a nervous gesture that caused his eyes to flicker upwards and an enlightened smile to dawn on his saturnine face.

'But of course...you don't want to get your hair wet—I quite understand.' His good-humoured resignation spoke of an intimate knowledge of the vanity of women. 'In that case, I'll be as quick as I can.' He turned her around and sent her on her way with a caressing pat of her sleek bottom. 'Meantime why don't you slip into something more comfortable? I'm sure you'll find the bed a perfect fit....'

Out in the hallway Nora put her shaking hands up to her hot cheeks. He was expecting her to be nestled on his pillow when he got out of the shower, eager and willing for another hot bout of mindless sex. Only this time he wasn't planning to restrain himself, and he had every reason to expect her to deliver the full bill of goods.

What had she been trying to prove with her craziness— that she had no more respect for herself than Ryan did?

She had never subscribed to the throwaway society. She

had secretly felt sorry for those people who drifted from partner to partner, substituting sex for emotional intimacy. And yet here she was, about to leap into bed with a total stranger. If she went through with this, Nora knew that she would utterly despise herself tomorrow.

She was shivering as she hurried back into the main room and scrambled into her own clothes, terrified that he was going to finish showering before she escaped.

She briefly thought about leaving him a note, but didn't dare take the time to hunt for pen and paper. Besides, what would she say?

Thanks for the mind-blowing orgasm, sorry I can't stick around to return the favour.

He was going to be furious enough that she had run out on him; there was no point in adding insult to injury by rubbing his nose in the fact. She couldn't even explain her behaviour to *herself*, let alone to *him*.

She snatched up her umbrella and bag and bundled her coat off the desk, her heart stuttering as she heard the low roar of the shower suddenly cease. Adrenaline pumped through her veins. 'Oh, God, oh, God, oh, God,' she chanted under her breath, darting for the door of the suite, shoes in hand. To her horror she discovered that Blake had flipped the security bolt when they came in and her sweaty fingers slipped on the shiny metal as she tried to disengage it without a betraying click.

Unfortunately, as she dashed out into the hallway, the inside door handle caught on the ankle strap of one of the dangling shoes, jerking it off her crooked finger. It banged against the wall and bounced back inside the room with a soft thump.

'Nora?'

Nora stared helplessly back at the stranded shoe as the door snicked closed in her face. It only took her a split second to decide to cut her losses. She ran down the hall and jammed the end of the umbrella on the button for the aeons that it seemed to take the lift to arrive, all the while casting panicked looks over her shoulder. He might glance out into the hall when he discovered she was gone, but surely he wouldn't bother to follow her? And, even if he did, he would have to dress first—that gave her at least a couple of minutes' grace.

A couple was all she needed. When the lift doors finally opened Nora blundered in, elbowing aside a clutch of Japanese tourists in order to take command of the controls.

For the price of a shoe, her freedom was won.

CHAPTER FIVE

NORA watched Kelly bounce out through the front door of their apartment building and down the short flight of damp steps to the footpath, her short shock of bright red hair glowing like a match in the bright morning sunlight.

Nora sank lower in the seat of her ageing Citroën, her hands whitening on the steering wheel, thankful that she had pulled in behind the line of parked cars near the end of the street to wait for her flatmate to leave for work…late, as usual.

Kelly was a PA in the public relations department at Maitlands, but her hours were hugely flexible thanks to the amount of social junketing with clients she was obliged to do.

When her previous flatmate had decided to move to Sydney a few months ago, Nora had posted an ad on the company's computer bulletin board. Kelly's outgoing personality and enthusiasm for life had persuaded her that the bubbly twenty-one-year-old would be fun to have around. It had only been after she moved in that Nora had begun to realise that their ideas of fun didn't always coincide.

She watched Kelly walk jauntily off towards the bus stop around the corner. It didn't seem fair that the hard-partying Kelly should be brimming with health and vitality, while Nora squinted through bleary red eyes, her mouth puckered with horrible dryness, her head squeezed in the vice-like grip of a vicious hangover. Of course, Kelly had been able to enjoy all the comforts of home last night, whereas Nora had had to make do with a depressing motel room and the spurious sympathy of a bottle of eighty-per-cent-proof vodka. And she didn't even *like* vodka!

The feeling, she had since found out, was entirely mutual.

As soon as Kelly turned the corner, Nora coaxed the Citroën's temperamental engine back into life and eased out from the line of cars at the kerb, driving down to slot into her usual parking place amongst the other residents' vehicles.

She got out of the car, moving carefully so as not to jolt her painful head, still brooding over the reasons for her enforced exile.

By the time she had reached her car last night she had been alternately sweating and shivering, almost semi-hysterical with relief. As she'd navigated her way through the saturated streets she'd vowed that she would never, *ever*, behave so irresponsibly again—no matter *what* the provocation. Or the temptation!

Operating on auto-pilot, she had instinctively headed for the security of her own home and had been shattered when she'd turned into her street and spied a familiar silver BMW parked outside the apartment and the lights in Kelly's corner bedroom glowing cosily behind drawn blinds.

Ryan certainly hadn't wasted any time, she had thought numbly. He must have left the party straight after Nora and raced over for more fun and games with Kelly. How many other times had the pair of them taken reckless advantage of Nora's absence?

Anger balled in her stomach. Ryan always liked to have the last word in an argument. What if he had arranged with Kelly to wait around and confront Nora when she eventually arrived home?

Home. That was a laugh. A home was supposed to be somewhere you felt safe, a protective fortress against the slings and arrows of misfortune.

And now that had been taken from her, too.

Nora had wanted to storm inside and scream at the pair to get out. The lease of the compact two-bedroomed ground-floor apartment had always been in her sole name, so she had every right to ask Kelly to leave, but she couldn't very well do it tonight—not in her current woefully vulnerable state; not until she had shored up her defences again.

She had several friends who would put her up, but most of them were friends with Ryan, too, and right now she felt too emotionally exhausted to run the gauntlet of the inevitable questions if she turned up distraught and begging for shelter.

So she had put her foot back down on the accelerator and sought out the nearest low-rise motel, a rather down at heel establishment which included an hourly rate on its dog-eared price card. Unlocking her door, she had noticed the neon-lit window of a liquor wholesaler across the road, in which a sexy female mannequin sported a sign promising a free T-shirt with every purchased bottle of famous-brand vodka.

When Nora had walked out of the store she'd been carrying not only the vodka and a black T-shirt but also the mannequin's fluorescent green leggings. She might have been stranded in the twilight zone but she wasn't going to spend a minute longer than necessary in the dress that had come to symbolise her stupidity.

And, having bought the vodka, it had seemed a good idea to stave off some of her misery by opening it. It would make a fine title for a reality TV show, thought Nora, as she opened the car boot: *When Good Ideas Go Bad!*

The vodka idea would certainly go down as famous in the annals of bad decisions she had made. She drank, but never to excess, and now she wondered why anyone would know-ingly court this kind of physical torture.

Carrying the company laptop she had forgotten to take inside when she had eagerly rushed home to try on her new dress, and with the rest of her things stuffed into the liquor store carrier bag, Nora nudged the boot of the Citroën closed with her elbow, wincing as the heavy thunk rattled her aching skull.

A tall solidly built man in a rumpled white shirt was getting out of a black van across the road as Nora approached the steps, her mind concentrated on getting to the top without her head falling off. The first thing she was going to do when she got inside was make a huge pot of coffee, she thought longingly.

'Excuse me?'

Nora looked gingerly around at the politely forceful voice. The rumpled shirt had a face to match—fiftyish, lived-in, blandly unremarkable except for sharp periwinkle-blue eyes.

'Miss Lang?'

She was trying to work enough fur out of her mouth to answer, conscious of his arrested survey of her vodka-touting T-shirt and bilious leggings, when he added, 'Miss *Nora* Lang?'

There was a hint of amusement in his tone which rubbed at her raw nerves. 'Who wants to know?' she said with uncharacteristic rudeness.

'These are for you.'

He held up the sheaf of red roses he had been carrying half-concealed at his side, and Nora was startled into feeling a momentary lift of her spirits.

Her mouth began to curve into an involuntary smile. 'For *me*? Are you sure?'

'If you're Eleanor Lang from apartment 1A.'

'Yes, that's me.' Her elation died and her smile inverted itself. Only one person she knew had any reason to send her flowers. She recoiled as if they were plague-ridden. 'I don't want them!'

He seemed taken aback at the heated response. 'Look— I'm just making a delivery, OK?'

She glared. Any colour would have been unacceptable, but red was rubbing added salt in the wound. They were even more offensive considering that Ryan had never bothered to send her flowers before.

'Then you can just deliver them right back where they came from,' she declared, her contempt recharging her dwindling stores of energy. 'And you can tell that—that *snake* who sent them that he's a moron if he thinks he can bribe me with a measly bunch of flowers! He's never going to get back what he lost. And when this goes public I'm going to make sure that everyone knows how it went down. Maybe people won't be so quick to trust him in future, if they know his personal morality stinks!'

She stumped up the steps, feeling slightly better for having vented her spleen, even if only at an innocent by-stander. The poor guy had looked quite stunned by her outburst. She glanced back as she went into the building and saw him walking back to his van with the rejected roses, cell-phone plastered to his ear...reporting his aborted mission, no doubt, she thought with a bitter sense of satisfaction.

Entering the flat, Nora felt none of her usual welcome sense of homecoming. To her dismay she felt alien in her own environment, tense and resentful of all the signs of Kelly's occupation—the open fashion magazine left on the couch, the unwashed dishes in the sink, the pile of ironing draped over a chair, the drips of nail varnish on the coffee table. Usually Nora was tolerant of her flatmate's habitual untidiness, but now her thoughtlessness seemed insultingly close to contempt.

It had been too much to hope for that Kelly had already started to pack up her things, Nora brooded as she switched on the coffee-maker, but surely she must have realised that she would have to move out? Until she did, the atmosphere in the flat would be hideously strained and uncomfortable.

A prowl around showed no evidence that Ryan had ever been there, but venturing into the bathroom made Nora's gorge rise and she hastily snatched up her toothbrush and re-treated. For the sake of personal hygiene she knew she'd have to get over her atavistic horror at the sight of her bath. Maybe she should get the place ritually exorcised!

A quick brush of her aching teeth and an ingestion of freshly brewed coffee made Nora feel a trifle less like dying. Anxious to change out of the tacky clothes, she paused to look at herself in her bedroom mirror and grimaced. Her eyes looked glassy and sunken and the stubborn remnants of her mascara deepened the bruised shadows that surrounded them. She had washed her hair at the motel, using the meagre courtesy sachet of shampoo, but the establishment hadn't run to hair-dryers and now her curls were an uncontrollable tumble around her pale face, her bleached complexion accentuating the ginger freckles and the faint whisker burns glowing on her cheek as well as on the skin above the drooping neckline of the baggy hip-length T-shirt.

She looked like a woman who had been used and abused, she thought bitterly—which was pretty much the truth.

Only…she had done her share of using, too, Nora reminded herself in a smothering of guilt. She had shamelessly courted danger and almost been consumed by it.

She kicked off her shoes and hooked her fingers into the waistband of the bright green leggings. Perhaps once she was back in her own clothes she would feel more like herself.

She tensed at the sound of the doorbell, and then relaxed as she told herself that it couldn't be Kelly—and Ryan also had his own key, although he had never given Nora similar free access to *his* apartment.

Nora's mood swung from brooding self-doubt to angry anticipation as she walked to the door. If it was that flower delivery man back again he was going to get himself a fresh ear-blistering.

She whipped open the door, eyes sparkling with challenge. 'Hello, Nora.'

For an instant she gaped, paralysed with shock and embarrassment. 'Blake! W-what are you doing here?'

He bared his teeth in a lethally unpleasant smile. 'Guess.'

She didn't like the sound of the sibilant threat and instinctively tried to whip the door closed, but that first instant of unwariness had given him all the edge he needed.

A muscular hand slapped against the wood and slowly applied the pressure to widen the gap to a full body-width.

'I—I'm just about to go to work,' she lied, struggling to resist the inexorable pressure.

His eyelids flickered downwards. 'Dressed like that? I doubt if it'll meet the Maitlands dress code.'

'How do you know where I work?' she croaked, the muscles of her arm straining against the losing battle with the door.

'I asked around.'

She wasn't fooled by the laconic drawl. Repressed fury oozed from his every pore.

'Where have you been all night?' he demanded, as if he had every right to know.

She tried to gather her defences. 'Look, I'm sorry I left the way I did, but I really don't have time to discuss it right now—'

'Make time,' he said, leaning more heavily on the door. 'I have something that belongs to you.'

Yes—her innocence. Before she had gone off with Blake MacLeod she had quaintly imagined that she could handle the kind of risk he represented. But she had never dreamed that danger would turn up on her own doorstep!

'I thought you might want it back…'

He was dangling something from his other hand, distracting her from his savage expression. Her wildly expensive new shoe. Shades of a fairy-tale romance…he had tracked her down to return her lost shoe!

A rush of relief weakened her grip on the door and, before she could register the unlikelihood of him performing such an extreme act of altruism he rammed through it, kicking it shut behind him with his polished heel. His head swivelled as he made a scowling survey of the room, seemingly unimpressed with the serenely comfortable decor which reflected Nora's unfussy taste. This was certainly no gallant Prince Charming come looking for his Cinderella. In a dark blue pinstriped suit and navy shirt and tie he looked ominously like a storm cloud looking for somewhere to pitch his lightning and thunder.

He turned to face her and Nora fell back under the frontal assault of his molten silver gaze.

'H-How did you find me?' She knew it hadn't just been a matter of looking her up in the phone book. After a number of nuisance phone calls the previous year she had obtained an unlisted number.

He pitched the shoe on to her couch. 'Your credit card receipt confirmed your name; the rest was relatively easy, given my resources.'

Her stomach lurched. He had gone back to the hotel boutique? She didn't know whether to be flattered or horrified.

'You thought I might have been lying about who I was?' she croaked.

'Well, I didn't think you'd really be fool enough to try and screw me under your real name.'

She stiffened, fighting a hot wave of shame. 'There's no need to be crude!'

His mouth compressed to a cruel line. 'Oh, there's every need. After all, what you did to me was the essence of crudity.'

She put her hands to her blazing cheeks. 'So I changed my mind—that's supposed to be a woman's prerogative,' she said, her words muffled with mortification.

'The hell you did,' he grated, stalking closer, deliberately menacing her with his size. 'You got me precisely where you wanted me, and I played right into your hands by acting the gentleman. I won't make that mistake again.'

She swallowed hard, dismayed by her body's response to his nearness. Surely he didn't mean to pick up where they'd left off last night? She ran her damp hands down the uneven seams of the cheap T-shirt.

'I—I don't understand,' she said, bewildered by his strange intensity. Why was he making it sound as if *she* was the dangerous one?

'Tell me, Nora, is there some personal history between us that I don't know about? Did I reject you at some point? Have I dated someone you know or slept with your sister—?'

She backed further into the room, wide-eyed with confusion at his sudden change of tack. 'I don't have a sister.' Only a brother who was living in Florida, well out of range of any screams for help.

'There must be something—some reason that you're willing to go to such lengths to discredit me,' he said. 'Is this some kind of vendetta? What's so important that you were willing to prostitute yourself for the sake of getting even with me?'

The heat drained from her cheeks. 'Vendetta?' she repeated shakily, putting a hand to her throbbing head.

She knew she had acted like a reckless idiot, but a *prostitute*? The accusation was too absurd to be insulting. 'I don't know what you're talking about.'

'Come on, Nora, a woman doesn't call a man a snake and threaten to ruin him without some very personal feelings being involved—'

'I never called you a snake!' she protested.

His face tightened in contempt. 'If you're going to lie, Nora, at least try and make it believeable—'

'I am not lying!' she shouted at him, almost blowing off the top of her head in the process, her slight body vibrating with outrage.

A sneer curled the corner of his mouth. 'Doug reported your conversation verbatim. You want me to call him up as a witness? Or was that comment about a bribe a hint that you'd prefer to be paid? Unfortunately for you, my stinking *personal morality* draws the line at giving in to blackmail. I'll see you in hell before I give you a cent!'

Nora had the strange feeling she was there already. She pressed a fist against her churning stomach as a light belatedly went on inside her fogged brain.

The man with the roses! 'I— D-do you mean—the flowers were from *you*?' she stuttered weakly.

He stilled, his eyes narrowing. 'You told Doug you knew who sent them.'

'I thought I did—I thought it was Ryan,' she murmured,

collapsing down on to the oatmeal-coloured easy chair. 'Why did you send me roses?'

'I didn't,' he replied bluntly, shattering any romantic illusions she might have been building up. He planted himself in front of her, hands thrust into his pockets as if to physically restrain himself from putting them around her pale throat and throttling the truth out of her. 'That was Doug confirming your identity without putting you on the alert. I'd described you, but he wanted to be sure he had the right woman before he let me know that you'd turned up. I'm not surprised he had doubts—you look like hell.'

He had no need to sound so pleased about it!

'That's strange, since I'm feeling so fantastic,' she said in a voice that dripped with sarcasm. She tipped her head back and glared up at him. 'Wait a minute. Are you telling me that you had this Doug person watching the flat, waiting for me?'

He seemed to relish her outrage, answering her question with his own. 'Your flatmate said you hadn't been home, so where did you go after you left me, Nora? Who was it you had arranged to meet?'

She bristled with hostility at the mention of Kelly. 'Nobody. Not that it's any business of yours! Look, just because we almost—almost—' She found herself floundering and he supplied her with a crude word that struck her like a bullet.

'—slept together,' she substituted with ragged dignity, 'it doesn't give you the right to come around here and interrogate me.'

'Would you rather discuss it with the police?'

'The police?'

He looked grimly satisfied at her dismay. 'You either deal with me or deal with them.'

He had to be bluffing! 'Are you crazy? It's not against the law for a woman to decide not to be sexually intimate with you...' She trailed off, remembering just how very intimate things had got between them before she had lost her nerve.

The extraordinarily vivid memories of their passionate encounter had haunted her all night.

'It is, however, illegal to steal,' he said harshly.

Thinking about the pleasure that she had stolen from him without giving him anything in return, she blushed. She had melted like honey at each stroke of his skilful fingers, selfishly absorbed in her own gratification to the exclusion of everything else.

'I didn't take anything you weren't offering,' she denied feverishly.

'Is that going to be your defence in court?'

'Oh, don't be ridiculous. You can't sue me for not giving you an orgasm!'

'*What?*'

He looked as stunned as she had a few moments ago, and Nora was drenched in scalding embarrassment.

She jumped to her feet, her uncertain balance almost sending her reeling into his chest. He automatically reached out to steady her and a hot thrill shot up her arm. She snatched it away, rubbing at the tingling skin, humiliated to feel her nipples firming and the skin along her inner thighs tighten. Oh, God, one night of almost-sin and she was turning into a raging nymphomaniac! What on earth had made her think that he was talking about *sex*? She closed her eyes and felt the room revolve sickeningly around her.

'*What* did you just say?'

Her eyes popped open to meet his darkly incredulous gaze. He looked as if he couldn't believe his ears, and she hoped that he wouldn't.

'I—nothing,' she mumbled, wrapping her arms defensively across her chest. She felt the whisker-burns he had given her glowing like brands on her face and breasts. *His* brand. She couldn't help noticing that, this morning, the hard jaw which had rasped at her skin was as smooth and glossy as polished teak. 'I guess we were talking at cross purposes. I'm not thinking straight—I had way too much to drink last night,' she admitted feverishly, by way of diversion.

'Are you trying to claim that you did what you did to me because you were *drunk*?' His deep voice was coldly scathing.

She wished she could blame the booze, but she wasn't going to demean herself even further. 'I wasn't *then*, no.' She pushed the curls back from her face with a limp hand. 'I only started on the vodka later—'

His eyes dipped to the inviting slogan on her T-shirt. 'When you were celebrating your successful getaway?'

'I wasn't *celebrating*, damn it, I was trying to *forget*!' Her stomach contracted with the force of her protest and she groaned.

'What's the matter?'

Desperate to escape from that laser-like stare, she clapped a hand over her mouth. 'I think I'm going to be sick!' She started for the bathroom, only to abruptly change course for the kitchen, as yet blessedly free of dire memories. Her nausea was nowhere as bad as it had been when she woke up, but at least she would gain a few minutes of precious privacy in which to regain her composure!

Unfortunately Blake appeared unfazed by the prospect of watching her vomit. He followed close on her heels, blocking off the only exit from the compact galley kitchen. Silently cursing him, she turned on the cold tap and ran it over her wrists, splashing droplets on to her clammy cheeks as she bent over the sink, cringing as the sun streaming in the window stitched a line of red dots across her gritty vision.

'You do look rather green,' he commented maliciously, resting his hip against the edge of the white Formica bench. 'But I thought it was just the reflection of those ghastly pants you're wearing.'

'Oh, please—don't try and make me feel better.'

Again, her sarcasm bounced off his impenetrable hide. 'There's only one thing that'll do that. They do say confession is good for the soul.'

She could never, in a million years, see him as a priest. 'Are you offering me absolution?'

'Retribution is more my style.' He let her see the volcanic temper still simmering in his eyes. 'Here.' He had rinsed out a used glass from the bench and filled it with water. 'The best cure for a hangover.'

Given his crackling hostility, Nora was startled by the thoughtfulness of the gesture. 'I've already had some coffee—'

'Water is better for the dry horrors. Drink it.'

Because she knew he was right, and she was feeling too rotten to dispute his right to order her around, she obeyed, taking small sips to spin out the glass as long as possible.

As she tilted the glass for the last drops, a tiny rivulet trickled down her wrist from her wet hand and dripped on to the front of her T-shirt. They both looked down at the silver droplets streaking down between her breasts and Nora saw that her stiffened nipples were tenting the thin black cotton. She flushed and something hotter than temper flared deep in his eyes.

She hurriedly clattered the empty glass back on to the bench. 'Well, if you'll excuse me, I really should be getting ready for work now. It's after nine and I was supposed to have started at eight—' She made a tentative movement but he refused to shift, trapping her in the patch of uncomfortably bright sunlight.

'I doubt it.'

Her mouth was suddenly bone-dry again. 'W-what makes you say that?'

'Because you've already phoned in sick this morning.'

'How do you—?' Her mouth snapped shut. He or his tame snoop must have tried to call her at work. This was what she got for being a conscientious employee! 'They're not supposed to give out that kind of information,' she said sharply.

He shrugged. 'I said I was your lover and we'd had a tiff… It's amazing how indiscreet people can be when they think they're giving romance a helping hand.'

'You *didn't*!' she gasped, then realised how naive and gullible she sounded. He had probably only been winding her up. Would she never learn? 'Oh, very funny!'

Her withering glare had no effect. 'Do you see me laughing?'

She made one last attempt at reasoning him out of his implacable hostility. 'Look, I admit that I shouldn't have run off last night, but I made a mistake—'

'And now you have a chance to rectify it. Give me what I want and I'll consider us even.'

Her stomach quivered. 'Y-You mean…here?' she squeaked. '*Now*?'

She had a fevered vision of him taking her right there on her kitchen floor, in the full dazzle of sunlight, sliding her against the hard glossy vinyl as he drove ruthlessly for the satisfaction which she had denied him last night.

'Yes, now. Before things go any further. That is, if they haven't already…'

The implicit threat in his tone nipped her torrid fantasy in the bud. The thumping ache in her head almost obliterated coherent thought, but she had sense enough to decide she wasn't going to leap to any more embarrassing conclusions.

'Perhaps you'd better spell out exactly what it is you want from me,' she said warily.

His eyes ignited under the scowling black brows, scorching her with his fury. 'It's a bit late to try and act innocent,' he growled. 'We both know you're as guilty as sin. I want the property you lifted from my hotel room.' He straightened, exuding a powerful menace. 'So, are you going to hand it over quietly—or are we going to have to do this the hard way?'

CHAPTER SIX

'*Property*—?' Nora broke off, a smile of relieved enlightenment dawning on her pallid face. 'Ohh—oh you mean *that*…'

There was no answering humour in his expression. 'Yes, *that*,' he echoed grimly.

'I told you I wasn't thinking straight this morning, otherwise I would have clicked straight away,' she said, embarrassed by her obtuseness. 'Of course you want your disk back…I'm really sorry for the mix up. I'll just go and get it—'

She moved, confidently expecting him to give way, but he didn't and she walked straight into his solid chest. His hands closed around her upper arms as her bare feet stubbed themselves against his polished shoes. She gave a little squeak as he lifted her until her face was level with his.

'Go where, exactly?'

'To my bedroom,' she gasped, conscious of her dangling legs bumping against his iron thighs, of the effortless ease with which he had lifted her. 'If you'll put me down, I'll fetch it for you—'

'Like an obedient little bitch? I don't think so.' His acid words were etched with cynicism. 'I'm sure you'll understand if I insist on coming with you. I wouldn't like you to vanish on me again.'

'For goodness' sake, what do you think I'm going to do? Climb out the window?' she protested shakily, pushing against his iron shoulders to little effect.

'At this point, I wouldn't put anything past you,' he said, setting her back down on the ground, but keeping a firm grip on one slender elbow.

'Don't be silly,' she said, hurrying into the bedroom, trying to ignore his overwhelming closeness and the electric tingle of his fingertips against her skin. 'It's not as if I *meant* to take it. It must have got caught up in the folds of my coat when I grabbed it off your desk last night. I was going to courier it back to you today—'

'Really?' He drew out the word into a sceptical drawl.

Nora had always thought her bedroom was airy and spacious, but as soon as Blake stepped through the door the proportions suddenly seemed to shrink and the oxygen supply dip below the level of comfort.

'It's not usually this messy,' she was annoyed to find herself explaining, hastily gathering up the scattered clothing from the rumpled bedcover. 'I—I left in rather a hurry yesterday.'

His all-encompassing glance had taken in the orderly possessions on her mirrored dressing-table, the neatly coordinated clothes hanging in the open wardrobe and the tidy row of photo frames on her tallboy.

'Are these your parents?'

'What?' She looked up from rummaging in the bulging side pocket of the soft-sided case that held her laptop to see him studying a photo of herself aged ten, flanked by a blond couple exchanging laughing looks over her nut-brown head. 'Oh, no, they died when I was little—that's my father's sister and her husband—Aunt Tess and Uncle Pat—they brought my brother Sean and me up.' Her voice was coloured with unconscious warmth as she attempted to take the edge off his hostility by adding, 'They hadn't planned on having kids themselves, so we were a bit of a drag on their lifestyle, but they never made us feel unwanted—'

'Do they still live in Invercargill?'

She stiffened. She was sure she hadn't mentioned her origins last night. He must have discovered it while delving into her identity. It gave her a shivery feeling to think that he knew things about her that she hadn't chosen to tell him. Not that she had anything to hide, she consoled herself. The fact that she had lived the majority of her life in a small town on the southernmost tip of the South Island was a point in her favour as far as she was concerned.

'Yes, they do. As I'm sure your paid snoop will confirm,' she said tartly, pulling out the compact disk in its clear plastic protector. She had been a self-deluded idiot to think for even one second that Blake MacLeod's unfinished business with her was anything to do with what had happened between them in his room last night.

He turned. 'A wise man knows his enemies.'

'I'm *not* your enemy,' she protested, slapping the disk into his outstretched hand. 'And I don't steal,' she added with all the force of angry sincerity. 'When I found this lying on the back seat of my car last night, I had no idea where it came from—'

He stared impassively down into her wide-set eyes. 'Copies?'

'I beg your pardon?'

'I want any and all copies you've made,' he said, slipping the CD into the inside pocket of his jacket. 'And don't bother to tell me you didn't burn any, because I wouldn't believe you.'

She gritted her teeth. He made it sound as if good computer housekeeping was a criminal act. 'Since I didn't know what the disk was, of course I made a back-up copy before I tried to open it,' she informed him.

'Is that where you were last night…at your office, downloading my confidential data on to Maitlands' network? I suppose you were hoping I wouldn't notice anything was missing until today. Unluckily for you, I decided to do some more work after you ran out on me—'

'Don't be ridiculous! I never went near the office,' she said tightly, massaging her aching temple. 'Why would I? I told you, I didn't know what the disk was, and I couldn't very well return it until I found out who it belonged to, could I? I happened to have my laptop with me, so I used that to check it out.' She found the copy she had made and shoved it at him. 'There. Now, feel free to leave after you apologise!'

Her bitter sarcasm had little effect. 'Did you make a printout or email it to anyone?'

Her generous mouth thinned. 'Of course not. And, no, I'm not going to turn over my computer to you—you'll just have to take my word for it.'

'And why should I do that?'

'Because I'm a very trustworthy person,' she snapped.

His steely gaze was unrelenting as it inspected her shiny face. 'You expect me to believe this was all an unfortunate coincidence…? That you didn't seduce me in order to gain access to information in my hotel room—'

'Any seduction going on was entirely mutual!' she choked.

A faint gleam appeared in his grey eyes. 'You have an odd idea of mutuality. Or do you usually get your kicks from picking up strange men and skipping out on them as soon as you've taken your own pleasure?'

She clenched her hands at her sides. 'I don't *usually* pick up men at *all*,' she rebutted fiercely. 'I don't go in for meaningless one-night stands—'

His voice deepened into a dark drawl that wrapped around her like black velvet. 'Then why did you invite yourself to my hotel room? Why did you lead me on the way you did…let me undress you, touch you, taste you…?'

She shivered at his evocative words, her skin prickling from her scalp to her toes at the erotic memory of his sensuous skill, her limbs weighted with a strange heaviness that had nothing to do with fatigue.

'Look, you've got your disk back and I've apologised; what more do you expect?' she said raggedly. 'Can't we just forget about last night?'

'No, I'm afraid we can't,' he said, with an implacable gentleness that seemed more threatening than his former raging temper. 'Because we both know that you opened and read those files—didn't you, Nora?'

His soft words made it more of a statement than a question and her gaze dropped to the item in question, her thick brown lashes screening the guilty expression in her eyes as she watched him pocket it with its twin. 'It was security protected.'

A sceptical sound rumbled in his chest at her evasive answer. 'R-i-g-h-t. And you're a hacker from way back. You're one of Maitlands' resident computer whizkids, constantly manipulating the interface between man and the sharp end of technology.' He flaunted his newly acquired knowledge of her background with ruthless intent: 'You took papers at Otago University while you were employed there, but you never bothered doing a full degree course—you'd already proven yourself in the market-place, hawking your software skills since you were in high school. Coming up against a good security block like the one on this disk would be a challenge rather than a deterrent to someone like you.' His cool contempt was not unmixed with admiration. 'Given the time, opportunity and Internet access, bypassing it would be well within your capabilities. So don't insult my intelligence by pretending to be an innocent fluff-head.'

She winced at the accuracy of his insight, his accusing words pounding into her tender skull like hot nails. 'OK, OK—so I peeked at your boring reports,' she admitted sulkily. 'I know I shouldn't have—but, well—it was a choice of that or the porno channel.'

'What in the hell are you talking about?'

His abrupt scowl made her regret her loose tongue. 'I—I stayed the night in a motel a couple of blocks from here.' The words dragged themselves reluctantly out of her mouth. 'I couldn't sleep, the TV reception was dreadful and the in-house video channel was playing adult movies, so I decided to pass the time with my laptop.'

Finding that her computer was still in the car had been the saviour of her sanity through the long lonely hours. She had welcomed the company of a trusted old friend, one who was endlessly entertaining and who had never let her down. And the mystery disk had been a convenient distraction from her personal problems. With a complex puzzle to focus on, Nora had been able to shove her own misery to the back of her mind, her steady ingestion of vodka muffling any whispers of conscience.

'A motel? What were you doing at a motel?' Blake's face had tightened with renewed suspicion, his nostrils flaring with distaste.

Nora squirmed inwardly under his accusatory gaze.

'It's a long story.' she muttered. 'A very long, very *boring* story,' she hastened to emphasise as she saw his eyes flare with curiosity. 'And it really has nothing to do with any of this...'

He put his hands on his hips, his sleek dark suit cloaking a lean frame that bespoke both immovable object and irresistible force. 'Why don't you let *me* be the judge of that?'

She felt too fragile to keep battling his bull-headed stubbornness.

'If you'll just get me a couple of aspirin from the bathroom, I'll tell you,' she stalled, directing him with a limp wave of her hand. 'They're in the mirrored cabinet above the basin.'

She groaned as he remained welded to the spot. 'Oh, for goodness' sake—I'm not going to run away as soon as your back is turned. I have a thumping great headache and I don't want to go in there right now, OK?'

'Why? Is there a body in the bath?'

His sarcasm conjured up the images she was trying so hard to scrape out of her skull. 'In a manner of speaking,' she said, rubbing at her bloodshot eyes.

'Explain.'

She automatically baulked at the rapped-out order. 'Can't you get the aspirin first?'

'Stop whining and start talking.'

Nora had never whined in her life. Infuriated by his intransigence, she exploded and gave him an earful of her stored resentment, drawing a graphic picture of the sordid events of the previous day and taking a masochistic delight in painting all the gory details of her humiliating failure to satisfy the man she had honoured with her long-time affections.

'Is it any wonder that I didn't want to come home last night? I'd be happy never to see either of them ever again, but we all work for Maitlands so I'm stuck with having my nose rubbed in my stupidity five days a week.'

There was a crackling silence. 'So what was I supposed to be?' he asked with a distinct edge. 'Your revenge on the straying boyfriend?'

'No!' The instinctive denial came from the depths of her femininity, but was tempered by her innate honesty. 'Yes—no—maybe—I really don't know.' Nora slumped down on to the edge of the bed, closing her eyes and propping her elbows on her knees, resting her heavy head in her hands. 'Maybe it started out that way, but I don't know what I was thinking by the time I—we... It all seems so surreal now, like a bad dream....'

She heard him move away and was conscious of him using his cell-phone, but was too tired to strain to hear the low-voiced conversation and when next she opened her eyes it was to see him crouched in front of her, holding out two flat white pills and a half-filled glass of water. Disorientated, she blinked, wondering whether in her state of extreme tiredness she had dozed off.

'Thanks,' she said, and downed them quickly, puckering her mouth at the chalky taste. 'That wasn't arsenic, was it?' she joked weakly.

He eyed her pale face as he put aside the empty glass. 'Have you given me reason to want to murder you?'

She smiled weakly. Even if she had gained his sympathy, his trust was obviously not so easily obtained.

'Not that I can think of. I just thought—well—you might feel that I'd insulted your manhood...uh, the frail male ego and all that—'

He stood, towering over her. 'My ego is very healthy, thank you...particularly after last night. There's nothing more flattering for a man than to watch a woman come helplessly apart in his arms,' he mused in that dark and dangerous drawl. 'So violently aroused that she melts all over his fingers like sweet hot honey, and moans his name like a sexy mantra as she shudders to her first climax....'

Nora's lips parted, but not a breath of sound trickled out of her shocked mouth, a wave of heat chasing away her pallor.

'Or are you going to try and dismiss *that* as a bad dream, too?' he goaded silkily, his eyes riveted to her upturned face as he watched the wild flush creep up to her hairline. 'If you doubt my veracity as an eye-witness perhaps we could try a re-enactment to jog your obviously deficient memory....'

She shot off the bed as if the sheets were suddenly on fire. 'Uh, I think perhaps I will go in to work after all. I mean, I have to face up to Kelly and Ryan *some time*, don't I?' she babbled, raking the tangle of curls away from her hot cheeks.

'You're obviously still feeling pretty fragile right now.' He cut ruthlessly across her hectic tumble of words. 'Do you really think you're up to the *challenge* of confronting them in front of all your coworkers?' His subtle emphasis on the provocative word triggered a predictable bristling of Nora's pride.

'Of course I am,' she insisted thinly, despite a backbone that went to jelly at the thought. 'After all, *I've* done nothing to be ashamed of!'

'Quite.' Her gaze shot suspiciously to his and met an expression of such bland innocence that she frowned.

The brackets around his mouth deepened into a smile that made her stomach twist itself into fresh contortions. 'In that case, why don't you get dressed for work and allow me to drop you off?' he offered smoothly. 'It's the least I can do in the circumstances.'

She didn't want to dwell on the circumstances. 'Thanks, but I have my own car—'

'If you drank the amount you claim you did last night, then your blood alcohol level would still be well above the legal limit,' he pointed out sternly. 'What would have happened if you'd been involved in a car accident this morning?'

She was shocked to realise that the thought hadn't even occurred to her. She probably shouldn't have been behind the wheel last night either, given the several glasses of wine she had consumed on an empty stomach, she thought, appalled at her criminal self-absorption.

'Statistically, most car accidents happen within a few kilometres of home,' he said, piling on the guilt. 'I'd be reneging on my duty as a responsible citizen if I let you get behind the wheel again.'

She nibbled her lower lip. Why did the thought of the ruthlessly ambitious Blake MacLeod as a virtuous citizen set alarm bells ringing in the back of her mind?

'Does this mean that you've finally decided that I'm not a modern-day Mata Hari?' she ventured.

He gave her a measuring look. 'I suppose that depends on what you intend doing with the information you've unexpectedly acquired.'

'Nothing!' she was quick to assure him. 'It's of no matter to me if you want to acquire a *dozen* shipping companies—' She broke off as his fierce black brows snapped together. 'What?'

'I find that rather hard to believe,' he said, 'considering that one of Maitlands' leading clients is the preferred bidder for TranStar Shipping—the white knight elected to fight off big bad PresCorp's attempts to acquire a majority shareholding.'

'Is it?' She spread her fingers dismissively wide. 'I don't have anything to do with the acquisitions side of the business; I'm just a technician. Is *that* why you jumped to the ridiculous conclusion I was some sort of spy? Well, you don't have to worry about it, truly—because I really wasn't interested.' She pinned him with a hopeful look. 'Actually, my memory is pretty hazy on *everything* that happened last night.'

'But what you do recall of strategic value you'll no doubt feel honour bound to pass on to your employers.'

She frowned at his sardonic response. 'Not when the information was obtained unethically.'

There was a moment of stunned silence.

'You can't be *that* naive,' he said, in a voice so dry that it crackled.

She was stung by his obvious incredulity. 'It's not naive to have principles.' The tilt of her freckled nose indicated her haughty displeasure. 'Maybe if you were more trusting of people you might find yourself pleasantly surprised by the rest of humanity—'

'Like you were, you mean, when you stumbled in on your boyfriend and his busty blonde cavorting amongst the bubbles?'

She took the jab with a sharp intake of breath. 'It must be really depressing to be so cynical and pessimistic,' she counter-punched weakly.

'On the upside, I'm rarely disappointed in my expectations,' he parried. 'Shall I help myself to a cup of coffee while I'm waiting for you to change? Or do you intend to cut off your nose to spite your face and spurn my offer of a ride?'

He seemed to expect it, so she took perverse pleasure in disappointing his jaded expectations. 'Give me ten minutes.'

His mouth twisted downward as he backed towards the door. 'Don't make promises you can't keep. Women aren't programmed for a quick turn-around.'

Fifteen minutes later she stalked out of her room, bracing herself for a snide remark, and surprised Blake MacLeod delving in the laundry basket which sat on the washing machine at the far end of the kitchen.

'What on earth do you think you're doing?' she screeched, visions of perversion dancing in her head.

'Folding your clean laundry.'

She snatched the lacy black 36D quarter-cup bra out of his fingers and threw it back into the overflowing basket. 'That's not mine; it's all Kelly's—*my* laundry is over there!' She pointed to the neatly folded pile of fragrant clothes sitting on the fold-down ironing board. To her horror, lying on top was a pair of white cotton panties figured with cartoon rabbits, a pathetic contrast to Kelly's sexy wisps of lace.

'I see...' His voice was smoky with speculation as he turned to survey her boyish figure in the narrow buff skirt and creased short-sleeved white cotton shirt that she had hurriedly snatched out of her wardrobe.

'What do you *see*?' She regretted the snappish words the instant they were out of her mouth. She didn't need to be told she looked less than her best. She tightened her clammy grip on her laptop and hitched on the strap of her shoulder bag, trying to summon the stamina she would need to get through the rest of the day.

'I see that you're ready to go,' he said with an evasiveness that was more annoying than any critical remark. 'Are these your keys?'

Without waiting for an answer, he scooped them up from the bench where she had tossed them and smoothly shepherded her from the flat, locking the deadbolt and escorting her out into the dazzling sunshine. Nora's headache instantly flared as the hot needles of light stabbed into her brain and she submitted meekly to the firm hand in the small of her back which propelled her towards a long, sleek, low, wine-red coupé with tinted windows parked against the kerb. Eyes watering, she groped blindly in her shoulder bag for her dark glasses, muttering under her breath as they eluded her grasp.

He opened the passenger door of the car and she sank gratefully into the inviting dimness, still rummaging in her open bag.

'Here, let me put that in the boot for you and give you more leg-room,' he said, removing her laptop from her feet and suiting his action to his words.

He dipped his head as he returned to her open door. 'What's the matter?'

'I can't find my sunglasses,' she whimpered.

'I'm not surprised, given the quantity of clutter you seem to cart around with you,' came the unsympathetic answer.

She gritted her teeth as she tried to think up a suitably

scathing reply, only to be cut off by his impatient curse as he straightened, his hand tightening around her keys.

'Damn! I must've left my cell-phone on your table. Wait here—I'll be right back.'

'See if you can find my sunglasses, too,' she just had time to fling at him before the car door was closed firmly in her face and he strode back towards the flat with an energy that made her feel doubly exhausted. She slumped back in the butter-soft leather seat and discovered that her fingers were resting on the elusive eyewear. She debated calling after him, but couldn't work up the energy to reopen the door. Serve him right if he had to waste some more of his precious time on a fruitless search. Nora slid the sunglasses out of her bag and on to her nose. She clipped on her seatbelt and lay back in the soothing dimness, waiting for the painkillers she had swallowed to kick in.

She closed her eyes, the better to brood on the iniquities of men in general and one or two in particular, and only opened them again when she felt a vibrating thud from the rear of the car. She discovered she had slumped sideways in her seat and hurriedly sat upright as Blake MacLeod walked around from the back of the vehicle. He had taken off his jacket and tie and must have stowed them in the boot. She wondered why he had bothered for such a short trip.

He slid in behind the steering wheel. With the collar of his navy shirt unbuttoned he looked as comfortable as she felt grotty.

'What took you so long?' she needled.

He fastened his seatbelt and started the car, ignoring the provocation. 'I see you found your sunglasses,' he commented over the signature rumble of a V-8 engine.

'They were in my bag all along,' she admitted with sweet malice.

'Why didn't you phone your flat and let me know I could stop hunting?'

'Because I don't have my mobile with me. I left it at work yesterday,' she shot back.

'Really? A technophile without her phone? Isn't that a contradiction in terms?' he said as he glanced in the rear-view mirror and executed a neat U-turn, sending the cluster of black-on-white dials under the steering column jumping.

She concentrated on adjusting to the unwelcome motion. 'I was in a rush to get home,' she remembered sourly.

'Lucky for you.'

'*Lucky*?'

'Ignorance isn't always the bliss it's made out to be,' her companion commented. The car pulled out on to the main road with a bellowing surge of speed that sent Nora's stomach lurching back against her spine.

'Would you mind slowing down a bit? I don't think I can take too many corners like that,' she asked through clenched teeth.

He eased off the accelerator and the car instantly responded to his command, the aggressive bark settling back into a guttural growl. 'Better?'

Sweat prickled across her brow. She swallowed the moisture that had gathered under her tongue before she answered. 'Thanks.'

'If you're feeling too weak to do this, I could turn around and take you back home,' he offered.

Too weak? So he no longer saw her as a sexy seductress, a proud Boadicea to his Roman general, but an object of pity? 'It's just the sudden change in direction. Keep driving—I'll be fine.'

'If you say so.'

'Don't worry; I'm not going to throw up on your expensive upholstery.'

'It's you I'm worried about, not the car,' he said, showing a stunning disregard for the possessive pleasure with which his fingers caressed the steering wheel. 'Why don't you just try to relax—take a power nap for a few minutes? Here, maybe this will help.' She heard a muted click and a delicious breeze sprang up to whisper against her face and throat, chilling the perspiration on her exposed skin. A soft burr signalled the loading of a CD and quiet classical music began to flow around the sculpted curves of the sealed cabin.

'Mmm, that's lovely…' Her smooth brow wrinkled as she pursued an elusive familiarity. 'What is it?'

'Ravel's *Pavane*,' His voice was leaden with patience.

'Do you usually listen to music like this as you drive?' she murmured.

He was quick to detect the trace of surprise in her tone. 'Do you expect me to be a cultural barbarian just because I don't have a higher education?'

Behind her closed eyes she mentally blinked. Did he carry a chip on his shoulder about his background? If he cultivated the image of himself as a ruthless savage in the business arena then he could hardly complain when there was a spill over of that opinion into his private life. 'No, it's just that it doesn't really gel with your public image. I expected something more…more—'

'Crude?'

'*Elemental.*'

'Gangsta rap, perhaps?'

She blunted his sarcasm with a yawn. 'Why should I think that? Was there a lot of gang activity where you grew up?' she wondered.

'You could say that.' Ironic humour replaced the sardonic edge in his voice. 'If you're one of those people who think official trade unions are legalised gangs. As for street gangs— yeah, we lived in a fairly rough neighbourhood, but I was too busy to waste my time posturing about on the streets. Dad was a hard-line unionist with no time for slackers—a rough-as-guts waterside worker who died on the job when I was twenty. Mum's a union activist from way back. There were four of us kids and we were all expected to pull our own weight from the time we were old enough to hold down a job.'

'You have three brothers?' It would be no surprise if he was raised in a swamp of testosterone.

'Sisters. I have three strong and opinionated older sisters,' he corrected, squelching her theory about his macho origins.

'So you're the baby of the family.' She smiled dreamily at a startling vision of Blake MacLeod as a chubby toddler bossed about by a trio of females. 'Do you still see much of them?'

'Too much. They live to complicate my life.' His wry affection congealed into irritation. 'Now, why don't you give that insatiable curiosity of yours a rest and let me concentrate on my driving?'

'Surely not difficult in a car like this,' she scoffed, her consonants slurring slightly as a pleasant lethargy stole through her veins. 'What kind is it, anyway?'

'A ninety-six TVR Cerbera—a classic British sports car.' He sounded typically male, shedding the hard-bitten cynicism for an endearingly boyish enthusiasm.

'Really?' Her eyelids were far too heavy to lift. She conquered another cracking yawn. 'I bet it costs a fortune to run.'

'You sound like my mother.'

Great! Now she reminded the most dangerously sexy man of her acquaintance of his *mother*! 'Cerbera...isn't that some character in Greek mythology?' she mumbled vaguely, hoping to redeem herself.

'Cerberus is the three-headed dog who guarded the entrance to Hades.'

'Mmm...hell and wheels—now what phrase does *that* particular combination of words bring readily to mind?' she teased drowsily, the leather of the padded headrest cool against her cheek as she sought a more comfortable position.

When he didn't immediately pick up the thread of the conversation, it slipped beyond her grasp. Nora's lightly drugged consciousness floated away with the music, weaving it into dreams, her weary body rocked deeper into the arms of Morpheus by the rumbling vibration of the car.

Her curls shivered in the breeze from the air conditioner as she slumped bonelessly in the cradle of her seat, her lips parted on a soundless sigh, her sunglasses sliding askew down her lightly freckled nose. When her companion reached out to tip them off and let them drop into her lap she didn't stir by as much as the flicker of a lash.

Blake's hard mouth kicked into a triumphant grin as he abruptly changed lanes and turned down a narrow side street. Snarling his way out of the prison of downtown traffic, he joined the steady flow of cars on the motorway and within half an hour was cruising on the open road.

Keeping a sharp eye out for the law, he exploited the road-hugging aerodynamics of the car as he wound up over the bush-clad Waitakere Ranges north-west of the city. Apart from the network of walking and tramping tracks in the dense native forest, the narrow dual carriageway was the only route to the isolated enclave of famously wild surf beaches on the other side of the ranges.

Blake's fierce satisfaction at the unexpected turn of events was charged with exhilaration. The Cerbera was a challenge to handle at higher speeds—a pleasure that he rarely permitted himself—but now he had the perfect excuse to put the car through its high-performance paces. Dust kicked up at the ragged edge of the sealed surface as he hurtled towards his destination, the leafy undergrowth and graceful ferns that fringed the roadside whipping and bowing in homage to his velocity.

The leisurely trip to his beach house from his home in central Auckland usually took just over an hour, but right now he wanted to get as far as he could, as fast as he could—before his unwitting passenger awoke to the fact that she had been hijacked.

Her story was so bizarre it was probably true, but there was too much at stake for him to risk giving her the benefit of the doubt. The fact that she had been pathetically easy to manipulate into assisting in her own abduction didn't automatically make her innocent of all charges. Unfortunately, at this point, wilful naivety could be just as damaging as malicious intent. Guilty or innocent, Nora was the equivalent

An Important Message from the Editors

Dear Reader,

If you'd enjoy reading romance novels with larger print that's easier on your eyes, let us send you TWO FREE HARLEQUIN PRESENTS® NOVELS in our LARGER PRINT EDITION. These books are complete and unabridged, but the type is set about 20% bigger to make it easier to read. Look inside for an actual-size sample.

By the way, you'll also get a surprise gift with your two free books!

Pam Powers

Peel off Seal and Place Inside...

LARGER PRINT
FREE BOOKS
EDITION

84

THE RIGHT WOMAN

she'd thought she was fine. It took Daniel's words and Brooke's question to make her realize she was far from a full recovery.

She'd made a start with her sister's help and she intended to go forward now. Sarah felt as if she'd been living in a darkened room and someone had suddenly opened a door, letting in the fresh air and sunshine. She could feel its warmth slowly seeping into the coldest part of her. The feeling was liberating. She realized it was only a small step and she had a long way to go, but she was ready to face life again with Serena and her family behind her.

All too soon, they were saying goodbye and arah experienced a moment of sadness for all e years she and Serena had missed. But they d each other now, and that's what

She held

Like what you see?
Then send for TWO FREE
larger print books!

YOURS FREE!
You'll get a great mystery gift with
your two free larger print books!

GET TWO FREE LARGER PRINT BOOKS!

YES! Please send me two free Harlequin Presents® novels in the larger print edition, and my free mystery gift, too. I understand that I am under no obligation to purchase anything, as explained on the back of this insert.

PLACE FREE GIFTS SEAL HERE

106 HDL EFU6   306 HDL EFVJ

FIRST NAME   LAST NAME

ADDRESS

APT.#   CITY

STATE/PROV.   ZIP/POSTAL CODE

Are you a current Harlequin Presents® subscriber and want to receive the larger print edition?

Call 1-800-221-5011 today!

▶ DETACH AND MAIL CARD TODAY! ▶

(H-PLPP-09/C6) © 2004 Harlequin Enterprises Ltd.

The Harlequin Reader Service™ — Here's How It Works:

Accepting your 2 free Harlequin Presents® larger print books and gift places you under no obligation to buy anything. You may keep the books and gift and return the shipping statement marked "cancel." If you do not cancel, about a month later we'll send you 6 additional Harlequin Presents larger print books and bill you just $4.05 each in the U.S., or $4.72 each in Canada, plus 25¢ shipping & handling per book and applicable taxes if any.* That's the complete price and — compared to cover prices of $4.75 each in the U.S. and $5.50 each in Canada — it's quite a bargain! You may cancel at any time, but if you choose to continue, every month we'll send you 6 more books, which you may either purchase at the discount price or return to us and cancel your subscription.

*Terms and prices subject to change without notice. Sales tax applicable in N.Y. Canadian residents will be charged applicable provincial taxes and GST.

If offer card is missing write to: Harlequin Reader Service, 3010 Walden Ave., P.O. Box 1867, Buffalo, NY 14240-1867

BUSINESS REPLY MAIL
FIRST-CLASS MAIL   PERMIT NO. 717-003   BUFFALO, NY

POSTAGE WILL BE PAID BY ADDRESSEE

HARLEQUIN READER SERVICE
3010 WALDEN AVE
PO BOX 1867
BUFFALO NY 14240-9952

NO POSTAGE
NECESSARY
IF MAILED
IN THE
UNITED STATES

of an unexploded bomb—one that it was going to be his very great pleasure to defuse….

A kick of anticipation tensed his muscles and his foot sank sharply on the accelerator. He had no doubt that once Nora recovered from her hangover her natural intelligence would reassert itself, turning her into a potentially dangerous opponent. But a fascinating one.

He glanced sideways at his dishevelled guest, deep in a trusting sleep. Far from disarming him, her vulnerability was unexpectedly arousing. Her shirt had slipped a strategic button and he could see a glimpse of smooth freckled skin above a white cotton bra, very different from the sheer black number she had flaunted last night. Perversely, he found the *faux* innocence of the opaque cotton even more of a turn-on.

A carnal image of Nora's pale body splayed out against the dark leather, her restless hands restrained by the tangled black webbing of her seatbelt suddenly flashed into his mind. It was so diverting that Blake over-steered a corner and almost clipped the crumbling clay bank.

Sweating and swearing, he spun the wheel to correct his mistake, shifting in his seat to relieve the sudden constriction in his loins. He was startled by the unruly reaction of his body to his erotic flight of imagination, and distinctly unnerved. He didn't usually indulge in fantasies of bondage and submission. His tastes were straightforward and earthy, and he had never felt possessive enough about any one woman to daydream about dominating her body and mind to the exclusion of all others.

This one was different. Unique in his experience. She had slipped under his guard with annoying ease: intrigued, amused, seduced, insulted and enraged him in swift succession. She had kicked him squarely in the ego and then had the nerve to appeal to his sympathies. As far as he and the rest of the world was concerned, Blake MacLeod had an ice cool head and a heart to match, but all it had taken to explode that myth in his face was one ruffled brown sparrow on an emotional bender. This morning she had caused him to act on an impulse that was guaranteed to create havoc in his smoothly run life…and, to top it off, she had almost made him crash his cherished car!

CHAPTER SEVEN

NORA OPENED her eyes to see a wall of green rushing towards her.

She let out a little scream before she realised that it wasn't the wall that was moving at breakneck speed. It wasn't even a wall... Where there should have been the familiar concrete canyons of the city there was nothing but a blur of trees!

'What's happened? Where are we?' She winced at the painful crick in her neck as she turned a bewildered face to search out Blake MacLeod's fierce profile.

'Nearly there.'

His thick brows were lowered in their characteristic frown, but his hard mouth was chiselled into a self-satisfied smile which rang alarm bells.

'Nearly *where*?'

Nora gave another smothered shriek as Blake hit the brakes and spun the car down a roughly sealed side road cut into the side of the hill—a road so steep that it was almost vertical, and so narrow there seemed barely room for the car.

'Karekare Beach is just over to your right.' He nodded towards the flash of glittering sea that revealed itself between the bisecting hills.

'How can it be? You were supposed to be dropping me off at work!' she squeaked, instinctively bracing her feet against the floor in the vain hope of stopping their plunging descent.

'I changed my mind.'

'You can't do that!' she spluttered, clutching the edge of her seat as he rounded another tight corner.

His eyebrow shot up in an ironic slant that said he already had.

Outside her window, the forest fell away into a steep-sided valley and Nora blanched, her heart leaping into her mouth at the sight of the flimsy wooden crash barrier that marked the edge of the drop.

'Oh, God!' she groaned weakly. The music which had earlier soothed her now seemed to mock her fear. 'You lying rat!'

'A pity you had to wake up during this bit,' Blake murmured with abrasive sympathy. 'But once we get down under the bush canopy again you won't notice the elevation.'

'Don't bank on it!' She sucked in a nervous breath that did nothing to reassure her. 'Is it my imagination or is the air thinner up here?'

'We're not *that* high,' he replied with an admirably straight face. 'You needn't worry about me passing out at the wheel from hypoxia.'

She shuddered. 'What happens if we meet someone coming the other way?' she fretted.

'One of us has to back up until there's room to pass,' he said, with a calmness that told her he had done this many times before.

Suspicion congealed into full-blown certainty: this was no random drive to blow away the mental cobwebs. 'Where exactly are we going, MacLeod?'

'Somewhere nice and secluded—'

'—where no one will hear me scream?' she concluded with acid sarcasm.

'Where you can take time out—relax and unwind in the peace and quiet of tranquil surroundings.' His deep voice mingled with the sexy growl of the car. 'No stress, no pressure, no prying friends.... You can catch some sun and laze about in luxury while you consider all your options....'

It sounded achingly like heaven to Nora's bruised soul.

'One of them being to have you arrested for kidnapping!'

'What kidnapping?' he countered blandly. 'I suggested we spend the long weekend at my beach house. I didn't hear you object, so naturally I assumed that you were willing....'

'How *could* I have objected? I was *asleep*!' she blustered, her outrage at his blatant manipulation of the facts ambushed by a treacherous thrill of excitement.

His beach house? The long weekend? She had forgotten it was a public holiday on Monday. She was on the brink of being stranded for *days* in Blake MacLeod's sole company!

She didn't flatter herself that Blake was whisking her away to his private hideaway because he was crazed by love, but there was a certain provocative undercurrent to his threats that charged them with erotic meaning. Even knowing that he had some devious ulterior motive for wanting to keep her isolated for the next few days didn't stop her from feeling a rush of feminine triumph. Boring women didn't drive sexy bachelors to reckless acts of piracy....

'You're taking a serious risk, you know,' she told him. 'I could cause you a heap of trouble.'

'More than you have already, you mean?' he asked, unruffled by the threat. 'Perhaps I believe that the potential rewards far outweigh the risk.'

She wondered what kind of rewards he was talking about. They hit a pothole and the car momentarily swerved, jolting her out of her abstraction. 'Why doesn't the council do something to fix this road?' she gasped.

'Because it dead-ends at a beach with no public facilities and there are only a few private homes along the way. The road doesn't generate enough traffic to justify the expense of regular upgrades.'

'Are you sure it's safe?' she gulped as an overhanging fern slapped the windscreen.

'As long as you're with me, Nora, you're as safe as you want to be....'

That was what she was afraid of! 'And if I said I wanted to go back?' She knew it was what she *should* say.

'To what? You didn't really want to go anywhere near work today. You were just saying that out of misplaced bravado.'

She gritted her teeth at the accuracy of the thrust. 'I was actually trying to get rid of *you*.'

'Didn't work, though, did it? Face it, I'm doing you a favour. Remember, revenge is a dish best served cold.'

'I don't want revenge.' She had wasted more than enough time and energy on Ryan already.

'Then you must be unique amongst human beings,' he replied drily. 'If someone I loved betrayed me, I'd take great pleasure in stripping them of everything they valued in life, piece by painful piece.'

Nora shivered at the icy implacability of his words and the implicit passion behind them. The kind of passionate intensity that had clearly been lacking in her relationship with Ryan.

'Maybe I wasn't really in love with him,' she muttered. 'He seemed like an unattainable god at university—he had a rugby blue and was hugely popular with everyone, whereas I was a geeky teenager who'd never even had a real boyfriend. Most of the other girls threw themselves at him, but I was too shy, so I—I—'

'Contented yourself with worshipping from afar until he deigned to notice you?' He sliced cleanly through her self-pitying gloom. 'Sounds like a normal teenage crush to me. I had one on my biology teacher when I was thirteen. It's one of those things you outgrow and laugh about afterwards.'

She tried, and failed, to imagine an adolescent Blake MacLeod in the throes of unrequited love. 'Yes, well…I was obviously a late bloomer. When he moved up to Auckland to work for Maitlands and suggested there was a job for me there I thought it was because he missed having me around. I guess I didn't really have a chance to grow out of my infatuation—'

'Perhaps because Superjock didn't want you to. I bet he

fed off your innocent admiration. How many people who challenged his superior self-image remained his friends?'

'At least I can blame my idiocy on youth and inexperience—what's *your* excuse?' she jabbed back. 'Why are you *really* doing this? I doubt if you normally encourage people to run away from their problems!'

He turned his head to study her, his gaze taunting. 'Do you really want to get into it with me right now?'

'Keep your eyes on the road, for God's sake!' she yelled, clutching the seatbelt across her chest.

He obeyed her ear-splitting command, scouring around the next corner. 'Sorry, but I like to look people in the eye when I'm having a serious discussion,' he said with pious calm.

'Then you can save the discussion until we get wherever it is we're going!' she gritted, knowing full well she was being manipulated. And to think she had been on the verge of forgiving him for preying on her vulnerability!

She simmered and suffered in burning silence until Blake pulled off the steep road on to a long, even steeper, concrete driveway which drilled down through the thick screen of bush covering the coastal side of the hill.

'I thought you said your house was at the beach,' she said nervously as the green canopy meshed overhead, further hemming them into the leafy shadows.

'It is. The beach is directly below us.'

As soon as the words were out of his mouth Nora's heart began to sink and her palms dampen. 'But, but—beach houses are usually at sea level…'

His mouth twitched at her choked protest. 'I prefer not to run with the usual crowd.'

'I knew there had to be a catch,' Nora muttered as the driveway burst out into blazing sunlight and she found herself looking down at the red-tiled roof of a semi-circular house which jutted out from the side of the hill. *Way* out…over a very high, very sheer drop.

'Oh, God...!'

'The structural engineering was done by a highly reputable firm,' murmured Blake reassuringly as they swooped down to the broad paved turning circle in front of three double-width garage doors. A short bridge fed across the falling ground to one side to a wide door protected by a wrought-iron grille. 'If anything, it's been *over*-engineered—the cantilevered beams are strong enough to support several times the actual weight of the house.'

He touched a slim remote and one of the wood-panelled garage doors silently lifted to allow the car to slot in beside a boat-trailer loaded with an inflatable rubber surf dinghy. Further along in the huge internal garage Nora could see a shadowy black four-wheel drive, a motorcycle, a beach-buggy, a stack of surfboards and a surf-ski next to rack of assorted wetsuits.

She debated refusing to budge, but Blake had already sprung open both doors and slid out of the car, and she suspected that sulking in her seat like a defiant child would get her nowhere.

Only when she had scrambled out and walked haughtily around the car did she remember that Blake hadn't needed a key to start the car—he had just pushed a black button on the swooping dashboard. Her heart stuttered and she tucked her handbag under her arm as she sneaked a look at Blake's bent head, half concealed by the raised boot. How careless of him! He really was taking it for granted that she would fall meekly in with his plans. She wondered if he would feel quite so smug watching her drive off in his precious car! The thought of handling all that power on that skimpy road made her feel even queasier, but a foolish rush of adrenaline sent her diving to pull open the driver's door. Her seeking fingers collided with a smooth unbroken surface as she suddenly realised what was missing.

'Mind you don't damage the paintwork.'

Nora jerked around to stare up into Blake's sardonic face. 'This car has no door handles!' she spluttered.

Blake smiled. 'A very useful deterrent to thieves.'

'Then how do you open it?' she asked, endeavouring to project an air of innocent interest.

'You could try saying *Open Sesame*,' he said smoothly, and she blushed at the reminder of their last ride together, in a lift.

'I think it's more to do with modern engineering than magic incantations,' she said.

His deep-set eyes gleamed. In the periphery of her vision she was aware of him sliding a hand up over the gleaming wine-red curves as tenderly if he was caressing a woman, his fingers briefly cupping the jutting wing mirror. There was a quiet click and Nora's bottom received a gentle nudge from the warm metal. Before she could react she had been swung decisively out of the way and Blake had re-shut the door and locked it with his remote.

As the garage door thunked definitively shut behind them, Nora zeroed in on the mirror he had so lovingly stroked and located the discreetly placed button beneath.

'Very cunning,' she said, torn between admiration and frustration. Just once she would like to get the better of him!

'I thought so,' said Blake, sliding his electronic control into his trouser pocket and picking up the bag, draped in his jacket and tie, which he had dropped at his feet. He strode over to punch a series of numbers into the electronic keypad on the wall, his lean back shifting to block her view when she craned for a look.

'Is that an alarm?'

'And remote deadlocking—it's on password access now,' he told her smoothly. 'Would you like to come in?' He opened the internal door to the house and stood back politely.

She lifted her chin. 'You mean you're actually giving me a *choice*?'

'We all have choices—they're just not always the ones we'd like them to be.'

'You have a very glib tongue, don't you?'

It was his turn to try and look innocent. 'That's not what

my teachers used to say. They said I was so quiet in class they hardly knew I was there.'

'I bet half the time you weren't,' she sniped.

His wicked grin was supremely confident. 'How did you guess?'

'You're the type to have problems with authority.'

'And what type is that?'

She wrinkled her freckled nose, the only part of her that didn't actively ache. 'Arrogant.'

To her chagrin he seemed flattered rather than annoyed by her insult. 'Is it arrogance to have faith in one's abilities?'

'If it gives you an exaggerated opinion of your own importance, then, yes. Conceit like that could be your downfall.'

'Now you sound like my father. He didn't have any faith in my personal vision of the future either. He hated it when Prescott offered me a job.'

'Did he think you should have stayed in school?'

He gave up waiting for her to move and brushed past her through the doorway. 'No, he just didn't like the idea of his son betraying his origins by becoming an errand boy to The Bosses.'

Lured by the skilfully dangled bait, Nora automatically followed, hovering by a potted palm in the tiled entrance way as he re-engaged the deadlock, brooding over his words.

'Didn't he want you working for Sir Prescott?' she asked, recalling the woman at the party who had mentioned the rumour about Blake's paternity.

'Let's just say that Dad disapproved of my capitalistic yearnings,' he said, with an irony that suggested a radical understatement. 'He thought that multi-national corporate executives were the corrupt robber-barons of the modern age. He would have preferred to see me pursue a career in honest crime than assist in the legalised oppression of the working masses.' He put his free hand under her elbow and guided her up a wide flight of stairs, their feet sinking soundlessly into thick wool carpet the colour of bleached sand. 'We fought like hell about it every time we saw each other.'

'That must have been tough on your mother,' she murmured, her bleary eye caught by the paintings which enlivened the lime-washed plaster walls—an eclectic mix of signed prints and originals.

Irony turned into open amusement. 'She wouldn't thank you for saying so. Mum loves a good fight. She and Dad scrapped like cat and dog all their married life. Being a MacLeod meant you learnt from the cradle to stand your ground and fight tooth and nail to defend your beliefs. We were all extremely vocal.'

'Except in the classroom,' she said drily.

He shrugged. 'I wasn't interested enough to make myself heard there, and since I worked before and after school I had to catch up on my rest somehow. Thanks to large classes and inattentive teachers I perfected the art of dozing at my desk—and it didn't cost me a cent in lost wages.'

'It couldn't have done much for your school grades.'

His mouth held shades of the cocky kid. 'It wasn't my academic record that caught Scotty's attention; it was my willingness to hustle, to tackle anything that was thrown at me, to persist until a job was done…'

His fascinating frankness, Nora realised, had been a deliberate ploy to take her mind off their surroundings, but now that they had reached the top of the stairs she was hit by the full impact of his private eyrie.

The open-plan living area was centred around a square firebox enclosed in glass, capped by a stainless steel flue and flanked on three sides by long couches in vibrant dark blue, deep-cushioned and luxurious. Bifolding glass doors and windows ran the length of the house, opening out to a wide sun-drenched terrace flanked by roughcast walls smothered in a dark creeper, the outer edge of which fell away with heart-stopping suddenness into a zigzag shaped swimming pool. An aptly named infinity pool, for beyond the shimmering sheet of captive water was…*nothing*…striations of blue sea and sky dissolving into an indistinguishable horizon.

Nora's scalp tightened over her throbbing skull, her whole body going rigid with alarm. 'There's n-no guard rail out there—' she stuttered.

'Yes, there is. You just can't see it from here. There's a strip of garden a metre and a half below the far edge of the pool, closed in by a solid balcony wall...' Which provided safety, but no security against Nora's soaring imagination.

Her lips parted on a soundless mew of protest but Blake had already turned her smartly in the opposite direction.

'Don't worry, I've given you one of the guest rooms at the back of the house,' he said, his hand flat between her shoulderblades as he propelled her through an archway on the other side of the stairs and down a wide windowless hallway into a high-ceilinged room with walls of palest coffee and Persian rugs splashed across the bleached carpet.

'See—' he said, crossing to the bay windows and whisking back the filmy curtains to reveal the dense native bush which formed a natural screen on the other side of the glass. 'No view whatsoever. You're tucked right up against the slope of the hill here. If you don't want to use the air conditioning you can switch on the ceiling fans, and there's a home entertainment centre in that lattice-wood cabinet. Your *en suite* bathroom—which is minus a bathtub, by the way—is through that archway. I'm sure you'll find everything very suitable to your needs.'

Suitable wasn't the word which sprang immediately to mind as Nora's jittery gaze fell on the queen-sized platform bed draped in white mosquito netting which dominated the room. Flanked by huge glazed pots sprouting luxuriant palms, the bed seemed to float above the floor on its polished wood pedestal, and behind the folds of the gauzy hangings textured silk cushions in jewelled colours and dense patterns were piled on the white bedspread, adding to the aura of exotic luxury.

Talk about Arabian Nights! Nora visualised herself languishing in sensuous abandon amidst the mounding of pillows, the silk cool against her hot skin, a temptress worthy of a sultan's favour…a tall dark grey-eyed sultan with a hawkish face and a black frown that made everyone tremble before him—everyone, that was, but the woman who could bring him to his knees….

'Well, what do you think?'

She blushed, tearing her mind from her silken fantasies, seeking refuge in cool flippancy.

'What—no bars on the window?'

He let the curtains drift back into place. 'Why should there be? I thought we'd agreed that you're a guest here, not a prisoner.'

His innocent expression fooled neither of them. 'You and I obviously have different definitions of the word "guest",' she sniffed. 'Which reminds me—you were going to tell me why you brought me here.'

'Of course. But why don't I let you get settled in first?' His grey-eyed gaze slid over her crumpled figure. 'You might feel more disposed to relax if you change into something more casual….'

He placed the small bag he had been carrying on top of the squat wooden chest at the end of the bed—and for the first time Nora noticed the distinctive home-made tags.

'Hey, where did you get that? That looks like mine!'

He gave a wry shrug and suspicion turned to fresh outrage as she elbowed him out of the way to unzip the lid and throw it open. A very familiar pattern of cartoon rabbits stared back up at her.

She flushed to the roots of her hair. 'You stole my laundry!'

He shrugged, unrepentant. 'I was being a good host. I doubt you would have wanted to spend the entire weekend in the same set of underwear.'

She was ransacking the contents, recognising several things that hadn't been in the plundered laundry basket. 'You went through my chest of drawers, too!' she accused.

'I thought you'd want a reasonable selection of your own things to wear. I know how women are about their clothes—'

'I bet you do,' she muttered darkly.

'Growing up with three sisters, I could hardly help but gain an insight into the female perspective,' he reminded her.

Her flush deepened. She doubted that his insight was solely due to sisterly influence. 'That's not the point. I didn't give you permission to go into my things—'

'Are we going to have an argument now over who first invaded whose privacy?' he drawled.

Her anger deflated like a pricked balloon. 'I already admitted that was a mistake,' she said.

'Which you're now going to rectify by behaving like the perfect guest,' he said smoothly.

'My laptop's not here—' she realised.

'Sorry, I must have left it down in the car—I'll bring it up later. Now, if you'll excuse me, I'm going to get changed myself. Meantime, feel free to explore. My room is at the opposite end of the hall.'

Was that a warning or a tacit invitation? Nora wondered with a shivery *frisson* that led her to close the door with a slight snap at his departing heels. Either way, her first inclination was to do the exact opposite of whatever it was he wanted.

However, she had no intention of cutting off her nose to spite her face, so she peeled off her hastily donned office battle armour and substituted an amber sleeveless T-shirt and a pair of loose white cotton shorts, both still fragrant with sunshine and washing powder, from her open bag. Then she ventured into the compact luxury of the *en suite* bathroom to splash water on to her face.

She nosed shamelessly into the drawers of the marble-topped vanity and found a mixture of used and new make-up and feminine toiletries of various brands. Evidence of sisters or his string of Insignificant Others? she wondered moodily.

Back in the bedroom, she couldn't resist crawling under the voluminous mosquito netting to find out if the bed felt as gorgeous as it looked.

It did. Soft, yet resilient, the mattress sank under her testing weight. Sliding her bare toes over the nubby silk, Nora experimentally stretched out to her full length, draping limp arms over the mound of cushions and letting her tired bones melt into the welcoming depths of the downy softness. Her puffy eyelids felt as if they had little weights attached and it was an effort to keep them open. Motionless, Nora became aware of the heavy silence hanging over the house, absorbing the continuous muted roar of the ocean and transforming it into a lullaby of white noise. Perhaps if she didn't move for a few minutes the warring factions within her body might make their fragile peace, she thought hopefully, and render her fighting fit for another round of verbal fisticuffs with Danger Man.

Her mouth curved into a bitter smile. Blake MacLeod might think that because she had let herself be temporarily swept away by his aggressive arrogance she would be putty in his hands, but she was no longer a naive soft-hearted idiot who trusted people to act with honour. No, she was a hardened cynic. From now on she would be a taker rather than a giver—smart and ruthless. And beautiful, of course…. She snuggled deeper into the gratifying fantasy of herself as a voluptuous sexy *femme fatale*, a fascinating woman of passion and mystery, an irresistible and unconquerable challenge to men everywhere.

And to one infuriating man in particular….

CHAPTER EIGHT

NORA DIDN'T BELIEVE in ghosts, but the white shrouds swirling around her in the smothering darkness made her rear up with a cry of alarm.

As she lashed out at the floating phantoms, the ghosts abruptly transformed themselves into billowing folds of mosquito netting dancing to the slow beat of the ceiling fan chopping quietly overhead.

She blinked and her vision cleared. Waking up in a state of horror seemed to be an ongoing feature of her relationship with Blake MacLeod, she thought wryly, batting away the wispy veils and scrambling off the wide bed. She could have sworn she had only closed her eyes for a few minutes, but her cramped limbs were telling another story.

Groping through the gloom, she located the familiar shape of a switch on the wall. The mellow glow of uplights sprang to life, but her relief turned to dismay as she stared at the dark rectangle looming behind the sheer curtains at the window.

She looked down at her watch in disbelief, verifying what her disordered senses were telling her. It was well into the evening. She had been crashed out all day!

A mortified groan rusted across her dry lips as she realised who must have turned on the fan. The thought of Blake looking in on her as she slept made her feel shivery inside.

Of course he had seen her asleep in his car, too, she

reminded herself—but his disciplined mind would have been totally focused on his driving. This was different—even though she was fully dressed, the surroundings were far more intimate....

Crushing down her embarrassment, she ventured out, following the faint sounds of a tap gushing and utensils clattering, underscored by some mellow jazz. The kitchen, she recalled vaguely, was at the far end of that huge open living space....

She marched into the almost dark room and came to a halt with a stunned gasp.

There was a sharp movement off to her far left, where angled halogen spotlights bounced off polished surfaces.

'What's wrong?'

Nora pressed her hand to the fluttering pulse at the base of her throat, a foolish reaction to the sound of his voice. 'Nothing... For a moment I thought there'd been some kind of volcanic eruption out there,' she said sheepishly. 'It looks like the whole rim of the earth is on fire!'

The wall of glass on to the west-facing terrace had been folded open, and far out in the darkness a thin line of molten red bled across the width of the sky, radiating hot colour up into shadowy clouds boiling with crimson, orange and gold: the last throes of the dying day. A velvety blackness, already pricked with stars, bore down from above, poised to smother the final rays of the red sun.

'Another minute or so and you would have been too late. The sunsets here are always spectacular—no smog to diffuse the light particles.' Even as Blake spoke, the last sliver of fire was swallowed by the black glitter of the sea and the hot crimson cooled to a golden-pink blush.

'I wish I'd had a chance to see it properly,' Nora murmured. When was the last time she had paused to appreciate the splendours of nature? Since she had come to Auckland she had allowed Ryan's scorn for such unsophisticated pastimes to stifle her enjoyment of the simple pleasures of life.

'There's always tomorrow night....'

The cool assumption in the gravelly voice spun her around.

Blake was leaning behind the curving granite-topped breakfast bar that divided the big kitchen from the rest of the room. With a shock, Nora saw that he was bare above the low-slung waist of his white drawstring pants. His raw masculinity was like a punch to the stomach, a violent reminder of the last time she had seen him stripped for action. A faint glistening of moisture dotted the dark hair on his tawny chest and imparted a glossy sheen to the streamlined muscles which rippled in the arms braced against the gleaming granite. Not an ounce of surplus body fat marred the ridged lines of his abdomen or the taut curve of his waist where it tapered to meet his lean hips. Nora hurriedly lifted her gaze from the tantalising streak of damp hair that arrowed down from the flat scoop of his navel to disappear beneath the loose gathers of white linen. The hair on his head was also wet, gleaming blue-black under a halogen halo and slicked back from his hard forehead to emphasise the dramatic widow's peak. The thick straight brows cast his grey eyes into shadow, but Nora could tell that he was amused at her flustered reaction.

'Excuse my state of undress, but I've just had a swim,' he said lazily. 'The pool is solar-heated but it's cool enough to be refreshing, if you want to take the plunge...'

Nora had the feeling that she'd already plunged in way over her head. He must have shaved very recently, she noticed with a fresh tingle of awareness, for the long masculine jaw was invitingly smooth and glossy.

'Uh, no, thanks.'

'I did pack a swimsuit with your things,' he continued as if she hadn't spoken, 'but you might prefer to do as I do and not bother with any encumbrance. There's no one overlooking us here, so you don't have to worry about peeping Toms—'

'Only peeping Blakes,' she said, walking self-consciously towards him, the soles of her feet shrinking at the change from soft carpet to the slick hardness of the unglazed tiles.

'Ah, but there's not much I haven't seen of you already, is

there, Nora?' he responded lazily, looking her over from sleep-creased cheek to dainty toes. 'You have nothing to be shy about, as I recall—you have a very nice body.'

She could feel her freckles popping at the blatantly patronising phrase. *Nice?* There was that damning, dull-as-dishwater word again. She had a good mind to peel off all her clothes and prance out into his pool just to show him that being *nice* was no longer on her agenda!

'Thank you, but I don't feel like a swim right now,' she said primly. Much less in a pool that dropped off the edge of a cliff!

He shrugged, a supple flex of his shoulders that drew her attention back to his tapering torso. Why had she ever thought that Ryan's thick and chunky rugby player's physique was the height of attractiveness? This man, nearly ten years his senior, had a honed sleekness which made Ryan's slabs of gym-inflated muscle seem like puppy fat, and a potently mature confidence in his own strength and sexuality which was more persuasive than any boast.

'How are you feeling?' he asked, and she ran a self-conscious hand through her rumpled locks, wishing she had stopped to look in the mirror before she had come marching out.

'Fine,' she said, pleased to realise that it was only a slight exaggeration.

She glanced around. The breakfast bar stepped down to a working bench that ran around two sides of the kitchen. Beneath the windows overlooking the terrace was a double sink and on the opposite wall twin ovens topped with a fearsomely professional-looking gas cook-top interrupted the smooth flow of the granite surface. Lacquered grey cabinetry complemented the brushed stainless steel of the appliances and hooded extractor.

It was a well-planned kitchen. One with a definitive style and a serious purpose. Just like Blake MacLeod. She would do well to remember that he reputedly never made an uncalculated move.

'I checked up on you several times through the day, but you were so deeply asleep that I thought it best to leave you to wake up naturally—you obviously needed the rest,' he told her. 'I only turned on the fan when I decided your skin felt overheated—'

'*Felt?*' Her tangled dreams suddenly rose up to haunt her. 'You mean you came in and *touched* me?'

The little shrill of guilty alarm in her voice goaded him to say innocently, 'You were very flushed and sweaty. I was concerned you might be suffering from more than just a hangover—dehydration can cause some nasty complications.'

Her imagination ran riot. 'You should have woken me—'

'As befits a Sleeping Beauty? I tried, but the evil spell of the demon drink must have been too strong.'

The riot became a rampage. 'You k-kissed me?' she said, her eyes instinctively falling to his firm mouth.

'Actually, it was vice versa. I just put my hand against your cheek and you grabbed me and wrestled me down on to the bed.'

Her hazel eyes jerked back to his, flaring with embarrassment. 'I did not!' she protested.

'You were all over me like a rash,' he drawled. 'I worked up quite a sweat myself, trying to fight you off without hurting you.'

She clutched at the edge of the breakfast bar to support her wobbly knees. 'I wouldn't! You're making that up!'

'How do you think I got these scratches?'

He touched a hand to the right side of his chest. Nora's fingers curled into her palms as she stared in appalled fascination at the four parallel pink lines scoring the smooth skin just below his flat brown nipple.

'You can examine me inch by inch if you like…. You branded me in other places, too,' he prompted softly.

She flushed, tearing her compulsive gaze from his hard chest. 'That doesn't prove anything. You could have scratched yourself for all I know, or it could have happened last night—' She broke off, aware of her tactical error.

He took full advantage of her confusion. 'Ah, yes…so it could. Some women are all teeth and claws in the sack, honey—here's proof that you're one of them.'

'We never got as far as the sack,' she growled.

'Until today.'

That was definitely mockery in his tone. Nora tossed her caramel curls, more certain of herself. 'Nothing happened. Or, if it did, it was only because I was having a nightmare.'

'It seemed more like an erotic dream to me—'

'And you would be an expert on those, I suppose?' she shot back unwisely.

Another distracting shrug of his superb shoulders. 'What can I say? I seem to attract women who like to talk to me about their sexual fantasies....'

A hot tingle streaked from the pit of Nora's hollow stomach to the tips of her breasts. She could feel her nipples begin to bud against the stretchy cotton of her bra and hurriedly hitched her bottom on to the nearest bar stool, planting her elbows on the granite and folding her arms to shield the front of her snugly fitting T-shirt.

Her apparent nonchalance was a dismal failure.

'You're starting to look overheated again, Nora,' he murmured, a thread of open amusement in the deep voice. 'Here, perhaps this will help.' He poured her a tall glass of amber liquid from a jug tinkling with ice cubes. 'I made it for you earlier.'

'What is it?' she asked suspiciously, curling her fingers around the frosted glass, keeping her gaze firmly above his neck as he resumed his former position.

'Iced tea,' he said.

She took a cautious sniff, then hesitated, with her lips touching the icy rim. 'Why aren't you having any?'

'Because I'm drinking something else.' He tilted his head towards a glass of red wine standing on the kitchen windowsill above the double sink.

Still she hesitated, and he made a rough sound of impatience. 'What's the matter? Afraid it's spiked? Do you really think I brought you here with the sole purpose of keeping you drugged and helpless?'

Her eyes widened and he gave an exaggerated sigh.

'I've already had ample time to have my wicked way with your unconscious self—remember? I try never to repeat myself!'

She felt foolish. But it was his fault for making her so jumpy. 'You can't blame me for being suspicious after the way you carried on this morning. How do I know what's going on in your devious male mind?'

He shot her a cynical look from beneath drooping eyelids. 'Oh, I think if you try very, very hard you could make an educated guess....'

She blushed. 'I—you—'

'Drink your drink and stop trying to pretend you're not as curious as I am.'

'About what?' she said, fighting to keep her end up.

'About what it would be like to finish what you started when you deliberately poured that glass of wine all over my jacket.'

Nora was tempted to bluff it out, but her conscience wouldn't let her. While she tried to think of a clever answer she buried her pinkened face in her drink. It tasted innocuous. She swilled more of the icy beverage over her tongue; in fact, it tasted quite delicious!

'You said you *made* this?' She gulped greedily, her parched mouth and throat absorbing so much moisture that only a trickle seemed to make it as far as her stomach. 'From scratch?'

'Don't sound so surprised,' he murmured, topping up her empty glass. 'I'm quite competent in the kitchen.'

He was much more than competent if he knew how to make iced tea. It wasn't a common Kiwi beverage.

'You just don't seem the domesticated type,' she said.

He turned to the bench by the sink where an assortment of partly sliced vegetables were strewn across the big chopping board. 'What type am I?'

She eyed the flashing knife, wielded with lethal precision against a defenceless red pepper. 'Rich single male—the type who eats out a lot and delegates all the grunt work to someone else.'

The knife turned expertly on an unwary onion. 'You think I'm lazy?'

'Quite the opposite. I think you're probably far too busy to bother with the mundane details of life.'

'Wrong. The devil is in the detail, Nora. It can make men's fortunes—or break them. The fact that I'm rich and single makes it more, not less imperative that I maintain my basic survival skills. Actually, I like to cook; I find it relaxing.'

To Nora, who found it a chore, he sounded insufferably superior.

'I suppose you're going to claim you do all your own cleaning, too?' she said sceptically.

'I'm self-reliant, not stupid,' he said, pausing to sample his wine. 'My eldest sister runs a co-operative of domestic cleaners—she gives me a good deal on a contract for my home in town and this place gets done for free, since the whole family uses it....'

A chip of ice caught in Nora's throat. 'Your sister's a *cleaning lady*?'

Her choking disbelief induced a grin that exploded the harsh angles of his face. 'Don't let Kate hear you call her a lady, she'll be insulted—she's a working woman. She started up a business which now supports her and her kids, not to mention giving other solo mums a chance to earn a decent wage without having to pay for childcare. I consider that a pretty admirable achievement, don't you?'

'Well, yes, of course it is…I just thought—'

'What? That because I'm wealthy my family must live in the lap of luxury?'

'It's a reasonable assumption,' she defended herself. 'Most people like to share their good fortune with their loved ones—'

'Not if the loved ones are pig-headed idealists who would throw the offer back in his condescending teeth,' he said wryly. 'You forget, the MacLeod roots are staunchly working class—I'm the renegade in a bunch of social reformers. Mum would take every cent I had for one of her causes, but for herself she doesn't believe in soft living or idle hands. She's a union activist who sees it as her duty to remind me that the average working Joe's health and welfare depend on men like me sacrificing a few points from the bottom line.'

A belated recognition clicked in Nora's brain. 'Your mother's the Pamela MacLeod who chained herself to an official limo during the Commonwealth trade talks in Wellington!'

'Actually, it was *my* official limo, and, yes, she managed to get herself arrested on primetime news. *Again*. Much as she's against the globalisation of industry she seems to have no problem using the information highway to globalise her fight against oppression. That artistic photo of her plastered against my grille was all over the Internet within minutes of it being taken.'

There was amused exasperation in his tone, a rueful respect that told her more about his feelings for his mother than any amount of words.

'She doesn't sound very oppressed.' Nora chuckled.

He rolled his eyes. 'I wish!'

She didn't believe it for a moment. 'Would you prefer to have the kind of mother who cooed and clucked over you and believed her darling boy could do no wrong?'

He shuddered—a very distracting ripple of that long, lean masculine back. Was he that same melted honey colour all over? she speculated helplessly. Her gaze slipped lower down his profile and she couldn't help noticing that the finespun fabric of his drawstring pants clung patchily to his damp flanks in a way that suggested he wore little or nothing underneath.

He turned towards her and her eyes shot hastily up to his face.

'Chicken.'

What was he? A mind-reader? 'Of course not!' She was embarrassed to have been caught sneaking an ogle.

He looked taken aback by her vehemence. 'If you don't want chicken, I could defrost some prawns…'

'Oh!' She fought down another blush, determined not to encourage the speculation stirring in his hawkish gaze. 'I—uh—chicken is fine, but really, I'm not very hungry—'

'You will be,' he said, cutting through her defensive babble. 'By my estimation, you haven't eaten in over twenty-four hours. You'll run out of steam very quickly if you don't put something solid in your stomach.'

At the moment the inner heat she was generating was enough to power a small city! Nora fumbled to pour herself another drink, her damp hand slipping against the handle of the jug, almost shattering the lip of the glass. 'Sorry,' she muttered, leaping to her feet as iced tea spilled on the counter. 'Let me get that.' She snatched up a handy cloth and mopped up the pooling liquid.

'Thanks,' he murmured. 'May I have my shirt back now?'

She looked down at the crumpled white cloth in her hand and noticed a button poking out between her thumb and forefinger. A tiny embroidered polo player, now stained with brown, stared accusingly up at her. 'Oh, God! I'm sorry—it was just lying there—I thought it was a dishcloth!'

'So much for my taste in clothes,' he said wryly. 'You really are hell on a man's wardrobe, aren't you, Nora?'

'I don't suppose it's a cheap knock-off rather than the genuine article?' she said with a sigh.

His trademark scowl wiped the amusement from his expression. 'Now you're adding insult to injury. Do I seem like the kind of cheapskate who would buy fakes when I can afford the real thing? Or do you think I'm just too undiscriminating to be able to tell the difference?'

'I think your inferiority complex is showing again,' she told him. '*I'm* the one who can't tell the difference. What do I know about designer labels? I used to sew all my own clothes before I came to Auckland, and I still get most of my stuff from chainstores.'

He cocked his head. 'Is money a problem for you?'

She wasn't fooled by the casual way he tossed out the

question. Her soft mouth tensed. 'Why bother to ask? I'm sure your snoop ran a full credit check on me.'

'And you came up clean as a whistle. But, as Doug pointed out, some debts don't show up on official files—'

'I'm not being blackmailed, I don't have a drug or gambling habit or any other form of secret addiction,' she declared, her voice rising above the smoky jazz. 'With me, what you see is exactly what you get!'

His mouth kinked, his gaze flicking over her slight figure. 'That's very generous of you, Nora, but I think we should eat first…'

She spluttered, as he'd known she would. 'That's not what I meant!' She glared in frustration as he carried the board of chopped vegetables across to the hob, watching him line up bottles of cooking oil, soy and sweet chilli sauce within easy reach of the wok.

'You're not going to cook like that, are you?' she felt compelled to say. 'What if the oil spits when you add the food? Here, maybe you should put this back on.'

He turned just in time to catch the balled shirt—thrown with a little more force than was necessary—as it hit his bare chest. 'Thanks, but I think I'll go and get myself something less clammy,' he said with a grimace.

She averted her eyes from temptation as he strolled past her, and while he was gone she decided to make the most of her opportunity to poke and prowl. She was rifling the telephone table at the top of the stairs when a voice sounded in her ear.

'Are you looking for something in particular?'

Nora jumped, her knee knocking against the open drawer, trapping her groping fingers inside.

'Ouch! I—uh—' She pulled her hand free and sucked on her stinging fingertips, flustered by Blake's sudden reappearance in a tight black T-shirt that was but a small improvement on the distraction of his bare chest.

'I was just wondering where the telephone was,' she mumbled.

'Why?'

'I thought I'd ring home...' she confessed, further unnerved by his looming intensity.

His eyes narrowed. 'You want to call your flat? I thought you said your flatmate had gone to work. Who was it you expected to pick up?'

She nibbled at her lower lip, presenting an unwitting picture of guilt. 'Nobody.'

The straight black bars of his eyebrows rose above eyes steely with suspicion and she sighed.

'I just thought I'd better leave a message on my machine, saying where I was and when I'd be back, that's all. You know—contact details in case of emergency.' She tugged at her wrist and his fingers tightened.

'You mean as insurance against any plans I might have to make you *permanently* disappear?' He invested his words with a silken menace.

'Yes—I mean, no! I'm sure you're a very law-abiding citizen,' she added hurriedly.

His eyelids drooped. 'I'm flattered by your faith in my honour.' His sarcasm was designed to intimidate.

'The phone?' she reminded him with dogged persistence.

'There isn't one.'

'No phone?' She was startled as much by what he said as his tone of grim satisfaction. 'But...there are phone jacks all over the place—'

'To be functional they have to be connected to a network,' he pointed out, stalking back to the kitchen. 'I come here to get *away* from all that—to have some uninterrupted down-time.'

Nora trailed after him. It sounded like an excellent theory, but...

'I don't believe it,' she muttered. 'I bet you didn't get where you are today by working nine-to-five five days a week. It would be tantamount to professional suicide for you to totally cut yourself off here, especially when your boss happens to be in the middle of a hostile takeover bid—'

'Which is why I regularly check for messages on my mobile,' he said, abruptly curtailing her speculative musing.

'Oh,' She felt foolish for forgetting. 'Of course. Then… may I borrow it for a minute?'

'Unfortunately, the battery's very low and I forgot to bring a charger down with me,' he continued smoothly. 'I'm sure you don't expect me to risk professional suicide for the sake of giving your untrustworthy flatmate a heads-up on your whereabouts?'

Nora mistrusted his bland expression. 'Then I suppose you'll have to drive me out to the nearest public phone booth so I can make my call,' she persisted.

His trademark scowl descended as he silently debated the extent of her stubbornness. Victory was sweet when he reluctantly fetched a slim state-of-the-art phone, bristling with all the latest software bells and whistles.

'Gee, thanks,' she said with a grin.

'Make it short,' he ordered, and flagrantly eavesdropped as she delivered her self-conscious little message to the answer-machine at the flat.

'Satisfied that I didn't pass on any state secrets?' she said when she finally slapped the phone back into his outstretched palm.

'You could have been speaking in code,' he pointed out.

She sucked in a frustrated breath. 'My God, you're suspicious—' she began furiously before noticing the provocative slant to his mouth. She lifted her chin and flounced past him to pick up her drink.

To her secret disappointment he meekly lapsed into bland amiability, delivering a smooth line in unthreatening patter as he expertly finished cooking the prepared food. He finally scooped the glistening contents of the wok into two white porcelain bowls and picked them up, along with his wineglass.

'I usually dine *al fresco*, weather permitting, but I thought you'd prefer us to eat inside,' he said, seating her at the polished slab of wood which dominated the dining alcove around the corner from the kitchen. Here the bifold doors were firmly closed, screened by wooden shutters slanted to obscure the view of the darkened terrace. Cutlery gleamed against the woven placemats grouped intimately at one end of the long table, burnished by the light from a row of tea candles in a tortured metal holder.

'You needn't have bothered to change your habit for my sake,' she said stiffly. 'I would have managed.'

He sank into the chair to her right 'It was no trouble.'

She bristled. 'Then why mention it?'

'Why, to make you feel indebted to me, of course,' he said, playing blatantly to her suspicions. He picked up his fork. 'And for the purpose of hearing you express your gratitude so prettily....'

Her freckles glowed, mini-beacons of mutinous embarrassment, as she shook out the paper table napkin and draped it across her lap. 'You're not exactly the most gracious of hosts,' she muttered.

'Shall we duel over our manners later?' he suggested. 'We may as well eat our food while it's still hot.'

The fragrant chicken was scrumptious, and after only a few bites Nora felt her spiky hostility melt away.

'This is really delicious,' she said, her voice an unwitting purr of sensual appreciation.

'I'm glad you like it,' he responded, watching her golden eyes haze with pleasure as she licked an enticing drop of spicy red sauce from the corner of her wide mouth. She ate with a delicate gluttony that sparked his own baser appetite.

'You missed a bit,' he said.

'Where?' she asked innocently, and he mirrored her actions with his tongue against his own cheek to demonstrate the spot. To his banked amusement, her gaze fixated on his mouth while a forgotten load of vegetables slid off her fork and landed with a splat on the table.

'Oh, dear!' She tore her gaze from his lips and jerked back, dabbing at the sticky pile with her napkin. 'Oh! Oh, no!'

'Don't worry about it,' he said, snuffing out the flaming edge of her napkin where it had drifted into one of the tea candles and ignited with a soft 'whuff'.

'I'm so sorry—' She frantically chased an elusive wisp of blackened paper as it broke away and floated in the air between them.

'It's only paper, Nora,' he said, capturing the ash as it settled into his drink. 'The napkins are *designed* to be disposable.'

'Not by incineration at the table,' she said, rubbing at the burnished surface, searching for scorch marks.

'Nora—'

'I don't think there's any permanent damage,' she discovered, thumbing up a tiny pile of soot.

'Nora!'

Her mortified eyes skittered up to meet Blake's winter-grey look of amused exasperation.

'Relax!' He pressed a folded replacement into her restless hand. 'Everything's fine. Just be thankful the smoke alarm didn't go off and bring the local volunteer fire brigade battering down the door. They're always eager to get some practice in.'

Her face registered a brief flare of horror before she realised he was teasing. 'I'm sorry. I don't know why these things keep happening to me.' She sighed, turning her attention back to her food.

'Chemistry. You're a natural catalyst,' he added when she looked puzzled.

'Should I take that as a compliment or an insult?' she asked wryly.

'Well, it means that life around you would rarely be boring.'

She pulled a face. 'That's not what Ryan said.'

'A catalyst is wasted on an inert substance. From what I overheard at the party, I would guess that *he* was the one with the boringly conventional mind. And the bathroom high jinks certainly suggest a sad lack of imaginative flair. A shower stall is so much more versatile than a narrow cramped bathtub—

as you would have discovered last night if you hadn't been in such a hurry to run off....'

Nora almost choked on a slice of red pepper and hastily gulped at her fresh glass of iced tea. 'Which reminds me, you still haven't told me the real reason you're so keen for me to hide out here for the weekend,' she said to cover her blushes. 'I wonder what it is you think I know that would make me a danger to you if I went back to Auckland?'

The seductive amusement was wiped off his face as he studied her brightly innocent expression from under lowered brows.

His long fingers toyed restlessly with the stem of his empty wineglass.

'I'll answer your question if you'll answer one of mine,' he offered, with such smooth guile that Nora almost grinned.

In fact, the knowledge that she was innocent of all his suspicions put her in a position of hidden strength when it came to bargaining with the truth. It was Blake who had secrets to protect.

'As long as it doesn't involve me giving you confidential information about my employer,' she stated firmly.

He gave her a bland look. 'I would never try to compromise your integrity.' At her disbelieving snort, he added, 'I have the greatest admiration for people who fight for their ethical principles.'

'Even as you try to circumvent them,' Nora murmured, although, strangely enough, she believed him. 'So, what's your *one* question?' She propped her chin on her hand, the reflection from the flickering candles creating dancing flames of mischief in her honey-brown eyes, her sharpened wits ready to repel any attempt at subtle trickery.

'Why are you afraid of heights?'

CHAPTER NINE

NORA'S BODY JERKED in surprise and her chin slid off the back of her palm, her teeth meeting with a sharp click that made her head hum.

'That's it? *That's* your question?'

'I'm curious,' he said, hooking one arm over the back of his chair, angling his body towards her, his eyes intent on the startled oval of her face. 'Is it a bad case of vertigo, or a genuine phobia?'

'I don't know what you mean by *genuine*,' she flared defensively. 'I'm not putting it on, if that's what you're implying—'

'I think you're confusing me with your *former friend*.' Once again he displayed an alarming ability to read her mind. 'I was in the glass lift with you, remember? I know you weren't faking that panic attack…although if it was a full-blown phobia I doubt that I would have been able to distract you as completely as I did….'

Nora suspected he was seriously underrating his sexual impact, but she wasn't going to pander to his already healthy ego by saying so.

'I thought that fake florist you sicced on me—'

'Doug is actually my Chief of Security,' he said.

'I thought *Doug*—' she pinched out the offender's name with disdain '—had ferreted out everything there was to know about me. Didn't he mention how my parents died?' Finding she needed to do something with her hands, Nora stood and began to clear the table.

'Only that they were killed in an accident when you were four years old—I assumed it was a car crash.' He circled her slim wrist with implacably gentle fingers as she reached across for his plate. 'Leave the dishes,' he ordered with rough impatience, tugging her around the edge of the table until she stood facing him. 'What happened, Nora?'

Why was she resisting? It was old news, after all…

She sighed. 'We were picnicking at a regional beach park and Mum and Dad went for a walk up a track over the headland. It was the day after some heavy rain and my mother slipped and went over the edge of the cliff. When my dad climbed down to help her they both fell to the rocks below.'

His lean face tightened with shock. His fingers slipped from her wrist to enclose her hand in a compassionate grip. 'My God, you saw all this? No wonder you were traumatised—!'

'Oh, no!' She was chastened by his shaken response to her stark description. 'Sean and I never saw anything—we were with my aunt at the far end of the beach where there was a sand-castle competition for kids. I didn't know the details until years later. I can't remember what they told me at the time. Sean was nine, old enough to understand what had happened, but I don't even have any real memories of life with Mum and Dad.'

'But you've been afraid of heights ever since?' She glanced yearningly at the dirty dishes, but he caught her other hand and drew her reluctant body further between his splayed knees. 'Nora?'

She sighed at the unyielding set of his jaw. This was the part she was *really* reluctant to talk about.

'No, only since I was fourteen, if you must know. It was just a silly overreaction…' She trailed off, but he waited patiently for her to continue. 'I went on a biology field trip with my high school class. I didn't realise until we got there that it was the same regional park. I'd never been back there, but

we were up on the cliffs looking at nesting sites and I felt this
compulsion to take a quick look over the edge—to—I don't
know—just to *see*.'

He leaned forward and she was aware of the hard column
of his splayed thighs, the utter intensity of his gaze, the latent
strength in the lithe body. It was both alarming and alluring
to be the focus of all his concentrated attention, almost as if
he really *cared*...

'So I looked down—and I saw—a woman was sunbath-
ing on one of the slabs of rock at the base of the cliff... She
was lying on her back on a red towel with her long hair
spread out around her head—for a moment I actually thought
that all the red was her blood! I didn't realise some of the guys
in the class had been rough-housing around behind me, and
right at that moment I saw her—' Her breath grew choppy.
'Well, do you know that silly trick where a person sneaks up
and grabs you around the waist with a violent jerk that seems
to shove you forward but really just rattles you in place—?'

Blake cursed, surging to his feet, flattening her captive
hands against his chest before roughly enclosing her in protective arms.

'Goddamned idiots,' he growled into the nimbus of curls
at her temple, his hand moving up and down her rigid spine.

Nora tilted her head back so that she could see his face,
his ferocious scowl brightening her heart. 'They didn't know
my history; they were just boys being boys. Any other time
and place and I probably would have been able to laugh it off,'
she said, striving to be fair.

'As it was, I totally freaked out. Completely lost the plot,
right there in front of the whole class. It was so-o-o humiliating. I knew what was happening but I just couldn't seem to
stop myself—screams, tears, throwing up—and worse...'
She bit her unruly tongue, dropping her gaze, hoping that he
wouldn't pick up on that mortifying detail. For a shy over-
weight teenager, losing control of her bladder in front of her
peers had been a deeply shaming experience.

'Anyway, I avoided high places completely for a while, but I eventually taught myself ways to cope.'

Going to university in Dunedin, she had had little choice—the city was much hillier than Invercargill and boasted a daunting number of multi-storey buildings. And, of course, by then there'd been Ryan to adore and impress…

'I can usually handle the anxiety OK now, as long as I get the time to psyche myself up beforehand,' she added. 'Thank God, it's never been as bad it was that first time.'

He looked down at her restless fingers, smoothing and re-smoothing his T-shirt, and slowly let his arms drift down to settle around her narrow hips. As he had suspected, the ruffled sparrow had the heart of a gamecock. When she was knocked off her perch she didn't lie in the dust waiting to be rescued. She rescued herself.

'Because you're no longer that young impressionable girl.' He brushed a stray curl back from her cheek, tucking it behind her neat ear, taking his time smoothing it into place until her skittish gaze darted back to his. 'Maybe your fear at the time was exaggerated by a form of post-traumatic stress—delayed feelings of grief and loss, especially the loss of your mother.'

Nora frowned at him, her hands spreading wide over his chest in instinctive protest. 'But Tess is the only mother I remember having—'

'That doesn't mean the memories aren't there.' His fingers had lingered on the sensitive skin behind her ear, toying with the lock of hair, his knuckles grazing her delicate lobe. 'Until you were four you were bonded to your birth mother, and then suddenly she vanished from your life. It must have been pro-foundly bewildering and frightening. You were obviously able to transfer your maternal bond to your aunt, although I notice that you don't call her *Mum*, or share her surname—'

'Sean still called her Aunt Tess so she thought it would be less confusing if I did, too. Lots of people call their parents by their first names,' Nora murmured, distracted by the little trickles of heat sliding down the back of her neck.

The strong supportive hand that had been in the small of her back had somehow moved south, his fingers curving down over the gentle flare of her bottom, the warmth of his hard palm tilting her hips against the cradle of his thighs, while her small breasts grazed his chest.

She struggled to pretend that she hadn't noticed, in case she was obliged to object. 'Anyway, Tess and Pat didn't formally adopt us, and Dad's father wanted Sean and me to carry on the family name—Dad was an only child.'

Nora's breathing was breaking up again, but not from the echoes of panic. That Blake was naked under his thin trousers was becoming more obvious with each passing moment. She could feel the unmistakable masculine shape of him against the hollow of her groin, the soft bulge of muscle slowly firming into a distinct ridge.

'What makes you such an expert on young girls, anyway?' she heard herself babbling wildly. 'I thought your sisters were all older than you.'

His fingers abandoned her ear to trail lightly down the side of her neck, his thumb dipping into the small indentation at the base of her throat.

'Four nieces.'

'Oh!' An unexpected laugh began to bubble up inside her, mingling with the intoxicating fizz brewing in her blood. 'No nephews?' she guessed.

He answered her with a mocking glower of discontent. 'My life is a plague of women. Kate's seventeen-year-old twins are reckless tearaways who need firm and frequent squashing.'

An effervescent giggle escaped Nora's compressed lips, unconsciously relaxing her guard. The new information had put the ruthless predator male in an entirely different light.

'Why are you looking at me like that?' he demanded

She had screwed up her honey-gold eyes, her freckled nose wrinkling. 'I'm trying to visualise you as a father figure,' she dared to tease.

'Oh, please don't!' His thumb flicked up under the point of her chin, lifting it to meet her punishment in the form of a smouldering gaze and sultry purr. 'Incest is not one of the sins I had in mind for you to commit…'

'I— Really? W-what sins?' she said, trying hard to maintain her brazen air and realising from his glint of satisfaction that she wasn't doing a very good job.

His head dipped, his face so close that she could see the faint throb of the blue vein on his temple and count the tiny green flecks that gleamed like buried gems in his eyes.

'Well, let me see…' he murmured, his warm breath caressing her flushed cheek. He swooped down to graze a soft kiss against her jaw, moving up to settle lightly on her pale pink mouth before she had time to do more than draw a shaky breath. Even braced for more of his outrageousness she was surprised by the violent kick of her heart when his tongue briefly slid against hers, only to withdraw with a tantalising flick that left her tastebuds craving more….

He now employed his clever tongue to even greater seductive purpose. 'I think lust, gluttony and covetousness are definitely on the list of our transgressions…' he nibbled suggestively at her lower lip '…with possibly a long, lazy stretch of voluptuous sloth afterwards. What do you say?' He rubbed his hawkish nose gently over hers, slanting his head to take her mouth with another, frustratingly light, languid kiss.

'Of course, if you're really hung up about the father thing,' he whispered, 'you could ask me to be your sugar-daddy—I'm sure we could arrange a mutually enjoyable exchange of favours….'

Nora's brief flirtation with sexual sophistication went up in flames as she wondered what favours he had in mind. 'Don't be ridiculous! I— You— Y-you're too—'

'Perverted?' he breathed into her stuttering mouth. 'Insulting?'

'Young!' she blurted, and went crimson at his deep

chuckle, a hot charge running through her nipples where they were pressed against his vibrating chest.

The sensation increased when his arm went around her back, only her braced hands preventing their upper bodies from melting together.

'Well, I confess I'd be a virgin in the role,' he admitted silkily, 'but there's a first time for everyone—isn't there, Nora?'

'Yes. I mean—no! I don't want you to play *any* role.' An X-rated vision of a cruel grey-eyed sultan and his languishing favourite suddenly revisited her imagination, causing her freckles to join up with rosy guilt.

'Shame!' His knowing grin damned her for a bare-faced liar. 'I could have delivered you an Oscar-winning performance.'

'For acting or special effects?' she muttered through her blushes.

He made another deep sound in his chest, half laugh and half groan. 'We do seem to have a rather special effect on each other, don't we?' The hand on her bottom moved down to cup one taut rounded globe, lifting her more tightly into the heavy fullness of his groin. 'What do you think we should do about it?'

She shuddered. The hot thrust of his desire ignited an answering fire deep within the core of her being. A molten heaviness gathered low in her abdomen, sending thick spurts of scalding excitement pulsing through her body, a turbulent mixture of fear and delight that threatened to burst the flimsy barriers of her control.

'I don't know…' She tried to remember all the reasons she should resist Blake's potent allure, but they seemed to be slipping from her increasingly hazy mental grasp.

He would be a dangerous enemy, but Nora had an uneasy premonition that he might be an even more dangerous friend! Despite all the suspicion and mistrust that lay between them, Blake made her feel things that she had never felt before, not even with Ryan. Her comfortable life had been thrown into chaos and the painful emotional upheaval was proving oddly liberating. She had *wanted* Ryan, but was beginning to realise that she had never really *needed* him....

'I can't think properly—' she gasped, arching her throat as Blake nuzzled into the warm crease of her neck, surprising her with yet another previously undiscovered erogenous zone.

'Then don't!' His rough urgency invited her to surrender to the moment. 'Just go with what you feel...'

But feelings could be treacherous, too. They put the generous, loyal and loving at the mercy of the cool-headed and self-serving. Did Blake even know what it was like to suffer betrayal on such an intimate level—to the extent that he could no longer trust his emotions?

Nora pushed her braced hands against the rock-hard chest, holding his overwhelming physicality at bay with trembling arms. She was right to be nervous. His harsh face was drawn into a mask of arousal, flesh stripped back from the bone, his mouth full and slightly reddened, a dark and hungry look prowling in the glittering grey eyes—the epitome of a dominant male.

'Have you ever made a total fool of yourself over a woman?' she wondered wistfully.

He hesitated, eyes narrowing, instinctively wary: a predator alert for hidden traps.

'No, no—of course you haven't!' she said, her voice wry. Blake might be an acknowledged expert in the bedroom but, discounting his teenage crush, he was no authority on love. He had been too well armoured by his ambition to allow himself to be sidetracked by his emotions.

'What makes you so damned sure?' he pounced. He seemed to have taken her answer on his behalf as a challenge. Perhaps he resented the fact that she could read him so easily.

'Well, you haven't, have you?' she said, the confident upward arch of her dark eyebrows making his own plummet to new depths.

A lethal smile peeled away from his teeth, baring his wolfish determination.

'Maybe that's about to change…' he murmured, contracting his powerful arms with an explosive jerk that collapsed Nora back on to his chest. He raked his open mouth over her parted lips, letting her feel the sharp grate of his teeth, forcing her soft squeak of surprise back down her throat with long, deep, drugging kisses that caused an instant sensual overload.

While the hot male taste of him ravished her senses and stole away part of her woman's soul, her mind spun sugar candy fantasies from his words. Was he implying that *Nora* might have the power to make him act foolishly?

Her heart fluttered up into her throat when she suddenly realised that they were no longer beside the dining table. His soul-stealing kisses had blinded her to the fact that he had been slowly walking her backwards, manouevering her with instinctive skill around the scattered furniture towards the plush blue couches that lay in wait in the shadows of the big room. At some stage her protesting arms had wound themselves around his neck, her fingers fisted in the cool dampness of his midnight-dark hair.

Dizzy and breathless, she felt her legs bump to a halt against the low arm of one of the couches, the plush velvety pile creating a delicious friction against the sensitive nerves at the back of her knees. She imagined being tumbled back the short distance into the safety net of deep squashy cushions, crushed into the softness by that lithe, hard body, dominated and controlled by his clever hands, which had already slipped under her T-shirt to explore her bare back and the satin smoothness of her seamless bra. His fingers looped under one narrow strap, dragging it to the side so that the cool fabric peeled down from the silky curve of her breast, exposing the taut button of her nipple to his rasping thumb. His tongue dipped and curled enticingly in her mouth as his fingers gently played with his find, drawing the delicate bud out to swollen fullness, milking it of pleasure with smooth, measured strokes, then squeezing with a ruthless finesse that made her shudder in violent delight.

'Yes, you like that. I know you do…' he affirmed with crushing satisfaction as he turned his carnal attention to her other breast, circling her begging nipple with a taunting scrape of his nails. He bit at her tender earlobe as he whispered, 'Do you remember how you felt at the hotel when I suckled your lovely breasts? You almost climaxed when I took your nipple inside my mouth. Shall we do it again now…?' His fingers tightened to illustrate his shockingly explicit words.

Nora thought she was going to faint.

'Oh, God—! No— I— Wait!' She panicked, teetering on the brink of a new emotional precipice, afraid, not of falling, but of actively flinging herself over the edge. Her hands dug into the thickly bunched muscles across his shoulders as she strove to cling to her fast-eroding resolve. 'You said you'd answer my question if I answered yours!'

His hands froze against her breasts. 'You've *got* to be kidding!' he groaned in her burning ear.

She shook her head, her curls bouncing against his cheek. 'We had a bargain,' she gulped.

He drew back. 'You'd really rather talk than—' He offered her a string of erotic variations that made her burn with curiosity. Was it really possible to do all those things? *In one night?*

She shook away the wicked thought and his mouth compressed, his eyes flaring with a ferocious impatience. She half hoped he might arrogantly ignore her shaky resistance, but instead she felt his whole body ripple with a series of pulsing contractions, as if he was fighting to rein himself in, muscle by individual muscle. His hands abandoned her aching breasts to encircle her smooth waist just above the band of her shorts, keeping her firmly compressed between his hard thighs and the soft side of the couch.

'All right, ask your damned question,' he said, with a clipped precision that signalled his rigid self-control.

She was dismayed to find that she was suddenly reluctant

to put him to the test. There were some things she might be better off not knowing…

'I just don't understand why I'm such a threat to you,' she blurted, aware from his rigid face that she was putting it badly. 'I mean, why hacking some stupid disk makes me so important. Because if it wasn't for that, you wouldn't have bothered to find me again, would you? Let alone bring me into your home. We wouldn't be here, doing *this*…' Her voice petered out as his rigid mask slipped to reveal a banked fire.

'Maybe not here and now, but make no mistake, Nora. *This*—' he rocked his flamboyant erection against her quivering belly '—would have happened between us sooner or later. Circumstances dictated the urgency but not the impetus…. You created that when you gave me that sexy look of wide-eyed innocence across a crowded room.'

Nora's body thrilled to his sensual threat, even as her mind shied at the picture his words were creating.

'Only it wasn't so innocent on your part, was it, Nora? You were marking me out for your experiment. And when the instant physical attraction between us went too far too fast, instead of dealing with it like a mature adult, you simply bailed.'

She squirmed, unable to deny it. But he was making it sound as if he had been nothing but a helpless victim!

'I hardly knew anything about you, and what I did know wasn't exactly reassuring,' she protested, discreetly wrestling her bra back into position over her tingling breasts. 'I'm not very good with confrontations—'

He gave a snort and she glared up at him in righteous indignation. 'I'm not! I'm usually very even-tempered and easy to get along with. But you have an extremely forceful personality, and it can be very overwhelming for an ordinary person like me,' she said, the spirited challenge in her glowing eyes unconsciously giving the lie to her words. 'Look at how you steamrollered over my protests this morning! And every time I ask you a question you don't want to answer you find a way to distract me—'

'When the stock market opens on Tuesday morning PresCorp intends to buy the rest of the TranStar shares it needs to take a controlling interest in the company,' Blake interrupted bluntly, shocking her to silence with his unexpected openness. 'We're confident we'll succeed in spite of the board's resistance because we have what we believe to be watertight deals with a couple of major stakeholders. The only way we can possibly lose out now is if a rival bidder manages to leverage one of our deals out from under us over the weekend, or can lock up a strategic shareholding by off-market lobbying of minority interests....'

Nora's eyes began to glaze as his frankness blossomed into talk of conditional bids and buy-backs and cross-holdings, but when he paused with a frown, she hurriedly rearranged her features to indicate intelligent life within. An ironic twist of his mouth suggested he wasn't fooled, and she was not to know that her glassy-eyed uninterest had done more to persuade him of her innocence than any of her heated protestations.

Fortunately for Nora he seemed to have finally arrived at the relevant bit—the bit that *was* interesting. 'PresCorp got the jump on everyone else because they expected we would wait to do due diligence before launching a bid, but we'd already run our own confidential investigation. That disk you took—'

'Innocently acquired—' she interjected.

'*Accidentally misappropriated*—' he allowed with a stern look of reprimand '—was loaded with highly sensitive financial information about TranStar, and PresCorp's share-buying strategy and tactics, and plans for future restructuring. There were also files containing some extremely compromising and potentially actionable personal material about past and present TranStar shareholders and directors. If some, or all, of that information were to leak out before we make our stand on Tuesday—even a *hint* that we'd had a breach of security and the knowledge was out there to be scavenged—it could wreck months of planning and create havoc in the market, not to mention damaging a number of reputations....'

'I see why your man Doug is such a favoured employee; you must keep him awfully busy.' Her vodka-blitzed brain remembered tedious graphs and dreary stock projections interlaced by screens of crackling-dry prose, but nothing of any personal scandals. She must have nodded off before she even got to the juicy stuff! 'You've actually *blackmailed* people into selling you their shares?' she commented incredulously.

A muscle flickered in Blake's cheek, but his voice remained cool. 'There's always cut-throat manouevring and mud-slinging behind the scenes in situations like this. Fortunes can turn over on a rumour. Grudges and loyalties get played out, especially in third generation family-founded companies like TranStar. Knowing who's sleeping with whose wife or who's over-extended himself buying a new yacht can give you an edge in negotiations. I don't break any laws, but there are always plenty of loopholes in the rules and regulations for the lawyers to dispute afterwards. Meantime everyone scrambles to protect their own personal positions and maximise their financial gains.'

'In other words it's every man for himself,' Nora said disapprovingly.

'Or woman. There are plenty of women out there ready to slit a company's throat for the promise of a seat on the board.'

'And you think I might be one of them?' she said, using scorn to disguise her stab of hurt.

His thumbs stroked her hip-bones, a glint of humour resurfacing at the sight of her furiously fluffed feathers. 'Somehow I don't see you as boardroom material,' he murmured.

More bedroom material? Nora bit the tip of her unruly tongue to prevent the old cliché from spilling out, but from the lucent spark in Blake's eye she might as well have uttered the provocative words out loud.

As an oblique form of apology it had bordered on a pretty good insult, she thought, trying to whip her hurt into a defensive outrage. She might not be brimming with management savvy, but she was clever enough to learn to run a company if she put her mind to it, albeit something small and interesting, like maybe her own IT business....

'So I'm here because you're afraid that my venal nature is going to get the better of me if I'm not under twenty-four-hour guard, and to make sure I can't escape with my ill-gotten gains if it turns out that I've already been corrupted! I'm surprised you want to sleep with me if I'm so obviously untrustworthy,' she said bitterly.

He met her stormy gaze with a compelling calm. 'There's a wider issue of trust involved here. I have to deal with the facts as they stand here and now, not as I want them to be. I have a responsibility for those I work for and with—a lot of people have put their faith in the soundness of my judgements. Every day they take huge risks based on my recommendations. If I start to make critical business decisions based on my personal feelings rather than best practice, then I wouldn't be worthy of their trust. And this buyout is set to cost Scotty several hundred million dollars, so he's not going to be very sympathetic if it all suddenly turns to custard and my excuse begins, "Sorry, but there was this bewitching young woman with stunning golden eyes..."'

Several hundred million dollars? Nora's stomach jumped at the notion. God, no wonder Blake was so paranoid! 'Personal feelings?' she ventured tentatively.

'*Extremely* personal,' he answered with a tantalising shift of his hips. His eyelids drooped, giving her a brief warning he was about to say something calculated to unsettle. 'And, by the way, Nora, I never said I wanted to sleep with you....'

'*Oh!*' Elation turned to instant mortification and she tried to wriggle out from between his thighs, only to have him bend to hook his arm behind her knees, sweeping her off her feet and up against his chest with a deep satisfied laugh.

'Because sleep will definitely be the *last* thing on my mind when I finally get you into my bed,' he concluded in a wicked undertone, carrying her across the room as if she weighed no more than a feather. He turned down the hall, adjusting her more securely in his arms, and Nora's head fell back against his shoulder as she contemplated her choices, knowing that there was only one she really wanted to make. Had wanted ever since she met him. This fascinating, infuriating, impossibly complex and wholly desirable man was like an elegant encryption, designed expressly to test her mettle.

'Where are we going?' she asked, her voice husky with nervous anticipation, convinced that she knew.

'My mother always taught me to escort my date to her door,' he teased in that same low, intimate tone.

Her door? Hadn't he mentioned *his* bed?

But of course every bed in the house was technically his, she supposed, her body suffused with warmth.

He set her down gently, in a slow, erotic, mutual caress of bodies, at the darkened entrance to her exotic room, and Nora willed her wobbly legs to support her as she prepared to take the scariest leap of her life. A leap into the dark. A leap of faith.

She swayed to meet Blake's lingering kiss, but when her hands moved eagerly up to cup his face he gathered them to his lips in a gallant, but chaste, salute.

'Sweet dreams, Nora. I'll see you in the morning,' he said, and with another brief goodnight kiss on her stunned brow he strolled back down the hall without a backwards glance.

CHAPTER TEN

THE THIRD TIME that Nora woke up in the big white-swathed bed on Sunday morning, it was with a smile of rapturous bliss. Instinct told her it was still early and her eyelids fluttered dreamily open as she rolled over on her side, reaching out to run a lazy hand over the sun-burnished body of her thoroughly decadent sultan.

Instead of warm bare muscles toned by energetic bouts of lovemaking under the hot Arabian sun, Nora found cool, crisp one hundred per cent Egyptian cotton.

With a groan of frustration Nora continued rolling until her face was buried in the depths of the smooth, undented pillow that lay next to her. She couldn't believe that Blake had once again sent her to bed with only her erotic fantasies for company. She was starting to wonder if he had any intention of living up to his bad reputation!

She had bounced out of bed on Saturday morning with the firm conviction that Blake's gentlemanly conduct at her bedroom door had merely been his clever way of ratcheting up the sexual tension between them. She had been sure that, having asserted his dominance, he would swiftly make good his sensual threats and seductive promises.

Instead she had spent the day with a man who had been by turns infuriatingly casual and maddeningly friendly.

He had fed her breakfast while chatting about the difficulties involved in the building of the house five years ago, and how it had been designed by the same architect who had built his home on Auckland's waterfront.

Afterwards he had given her a guided tour of the sprawling upper level, whisking her in and out of his aggressively masculine bedroom without a single suggestive comment, seemingly more interested in her opinion of the architecture and furnishings than in seduction.

Then he had chivvied her into changing and going for a run with him along the beach, taking her down the winding gravel road in the jaunty beach-buggy.

'My nieces tortured me into buying this!' he shouted above the roar of the engine and the wind in their ears as they shot on to the beach, but Nora could tell from the white grin that gashed the hard face below the black wrap-around sunglasses that he hadn't taken much persuading.

The tide was only halfway up the wide sweep of black sand and apart from a few hardened surfers out amongst the waves the beach was empty but for a family with a dog out on the rocks by the point.

They jogged the kilometre or so to one end of the beach on the hard-packed sand just below the high-water mark, but when they got back to the dune where he had parked the buggy, and Blake showed no signs of stopping, Nora collapsed panting into the sand and waved him on. With an insufferably superior grin he took off towards the other end of the beach at double their speed and did another couple of complete laps of the beach in the same pounding rhythm, while Nora fetched a towel and water bottle from the bag he had stowed in the cockpit of the buggy. Kicking off her sneakers, she stripped down to her pale bronze bathing suit, a sleek one-piece with a deep V neckline and detail around the high-cut hips.

When Blake returned, his tank top and shorts clinging to his sweat-soaked body, it was to find Nora sitting on a towel absorbed in conversation with a sun-bleached young surfer who stood, his wetsuit peeled down to his waist, his muscled arm holding his upright board to one side of his smooth, deeply tanned torso.

'Steve.' Blake's voice was as curt as his nod.

'Blake.' The surfie nodded back, grinning down at Nora.

'Going out?' Blake demanded even more curtly.

'Coming in.' The flick of a calculated hand through his long blond hair made Nora gasp as a glittering arc of cold drops splattered over her hot skin and slid down between her breasts.

'Sorry. Shall I lick that off for you, darlin'?' he offered with a playful grin that had her smothering a giggle.

Blake took a menacing step closer. 'Beat it, kid. You're playing out of your league. Especially if you want that summer internship you've been pestering me for….'

The fearless grin widened. Steve tipped a wink at Nora as he tucked his surfboard back under his arm with a flourish and lowered his voice to a stage whisper. 'Just remember, I'm the first on the left going up the road if the old man pegs out on you—I have a soft bed, a great stereo and a fully stocked drinks cabinet….'

Nora turned her stifled giggle into a choked cough as the young man sauntered on his way up the beach.

'You didn't have to be so rude,' she chided. 'He was just being friendly.'

'I suppose you were so busy simpering up at him you didn't notice he was leering down your suit,' he said tersely. 'You do realise that's his *parents'* liquor cabinet he's boasting about!'

Secretly encouraged by his dog-in-the-manger attitude, Nora stretched her legs out in front of her and leaned nonchalantly back on her braced arms.

'So he said.'

'Did he? What else did he say?' He dropped to his knees, removing his tank top and mopping his forehead, throat and chest with it. His brows twitched together. 'What were you two talking about?'

'I was telling him all your TranStar secrets, of course,' she said sweetly. 'We were plotting a way to get rid of you and take over the company ourselves.'

The snatched eyebrows melted into a laugh. 'Did you happen to mention I'd brought you here against your will and beg him to take you back to Auckland? I mean, this was your big chance to escape my wicked clutches and cause me maximum pain and embarrassment.'

Wicked? If only!

'I— He— As you pointed out, he's only a boy. It wouldn't have been fair to involve him,' she floundered, trying to disguise the betraying fact that it hadn't even occurred to her. 'And, anyway, since you're neighbours and he's obviously applied to you for some sort of holiday job, I doubt he would have risked crossing you—'

'But you didn't know that when you spoke to him.' Blake twisted the top off a second water bottle and she watched, fascinated, the rippling of his strong throat as he drank. Then he tilted his jaw to one side and splashed·some of the water down on to his sweaty chest, causing the skin to tighten and his nipples to visibly contract. The muscles in Nora's arms went lax, and to hide her sudden weakness she lay flat on her back, wriggling her bottom to form a comfortable hollow in the sand beneath the towel.

Blake froze, the bottle still held high, watching the shimmy of her hips and the matching shimmer of her breasts against the thin covering of Lycra.

'The colour of that suit is almost the same shade as your freckles. From a distance you look as if you're not wearing anything at all.'

She forced herself not to move. 'I do not!'

'How do you know?' he goaded. 'I bet that's why Steve came hotfooting over—he thought you were sunbathing in the nude. Did he look wildly disappointed when he got up close?'

'No, he didn't!' she gritted, although, come to think of it, he had given her a rather sheepish grin. 'I've had this suit for ages; no one's mentioned anything before—'

'Maybe lover boy enjoyed the view too much.'

'We hardly ever went to the beach together—or the pool,' she recalled. 'Ryan doesn't like swimming.'

'Except in bathtubs.' He took another cool swig of water. 'I forget, was it the breast-stroke he was doing—or the crawl?'

Nora's voice suddenly trembled on the verge of a laugh and her riposte was correspondingly weak. 'You're an insensitive pig!'

'And he apparently never cared enough to do with you the things that *you* liked to do. You're a genuine water-baby, aren't you? Doug said that you used to swim as a teenager and you still do lengths at the local pool several times a week, summer and winter.'

'I only took it up because I wanted to lose weight,' she found herself confessing. 'And then I kept on because I loved it—the swimming part, I mean, not the competing.'

'I didn't see it at first because of that ghastly dress you were wearing,' he said, 'but you have the classic swimmer's body—strong shoulders, high breasts, slim hips and long slender legs that look as if they have a real kick in them.'

He was leaning over, his shadow falling across her like a cool, dark caress, and for a shattering moment Nora hoped he was actually going to follow through on his softly flattering words but he suddenly rocked back on his haunches and jack-knifed to his feet, tossing the water bottle into the sand.

'I usually cool off in the surf after a beach run.' He started towards the line of breakers, casting a careless invitation over his shoulder. 'Join me if you want to give that suit a workout....'

His tantalising advance and retreat set the scene for the entire day. They spent the morning on the beach and went back up to the house for a lunch which meandered into mid-afternoon, then lazed around on the terrace, with Nora in a sun-lounger firmly wedged up against the glass doors of the house, her heart in her mouth every time Blake rolled indolently into the pool to disport like a seal in the silky blue water. Envy and a much fiercer emotion burned in her breast, but no amount of subtle encouragement or needling, or outright flirting on Nora's part, succeeded in provoking the desired response. His eyes intermittently smouldered with banked fire and he made plenty of excuses to touch her, but any impulse to turn the fleeting contact into anything more intimate was firmly diverted into conversational channels.

Not that Nora was bored. She learned all about his mother and his sisters—thirty-seven-year-old Kate and her Terrible Twins, whose father had dropped out of sight before they were even born; Maria, the thirty-five-year-old union lawyer who resided with her live-in lover and was following in her mother's activist footsteps, delighting at nipping at her brother's corporate heels; and his youngest sister, Sara, who worked at the restaurant managed by her husband, and whose two daughters were sports mad.

'I don't know why you need nephews; it sounds like the family females have all the bases covered,' she kidded.

'It'd be nice to have at least *one* of the next generation of MacLeods who sees the world from my perspective,' he said wryly.

'Well, it's obviously being left up to you to provide the masculine branches on the family tree.'

Something shifted behind the hawkish features, the steel-grey eyes darkening as they registered a seismic shift in his perceptions, then the cynical mask snapped back into place. 'Wondering if I've left any stray twigs lying around, Nora? I haven't, I assure you—I take *all* my responsibilities seriously.'

It was only natural that Blake's relaxed talk of his assorted relatives should lead Nora into comparisons with her own family, and stories of growing up in Invercargill and how Tess had been a great substitute mother, just not very domesticated. While her aunt and uncle were busy running their sales business it had fallen to Nora to manage the family household and do most of the shopping and cooking.

She was eager to boast about Sean, especially when Blake showed a genuine interest in her brother's career as a marine salvage diver and sometime Caribbean treasure-hunter. Over pre-dinner cocktails she confided that Sean's tales of his treasure-seeking expeditions had inspired her to start designing a computer programme which would help him more accurately predict the break-up and dispersion pattern of ancient wrecks in any given combination of sea-floor topography and wind and sea currents. Chin propped on his hand, Blake listened with such rapt absorption to her enthusiastic description of her ideas that she stopped worrying about his unfathomable behaviour and gave in to the sheer joy of being in his company, licensing herself to ignore the whispered warnings from her vulnerable heart.

Cocktails flowed almost seamlessly into another delicious home-cooked dinner, but in spite of Nora rifling her meagre cache of clothes for her one and only dress—a simple floral wraparound with a flirty flimsy skirt—the combination of excess sun, sea, fresh air and nervous tension took their inevitable toll and she actually yawned when Blake walked her along to her room and took her tightly in his arms.

He had *finally* got around to kissing her again and Nora had *yawned*! Worse still, instead of being offended or annoyed, he had *laughed*....

Nora groaned more deeply into the pillow, pounding it with her fists and kicking her feet against the confines of the top sheet, which had been tangled into damp skeins by her sweaty, dream-shot night.

Her mini tantrum over, she went into the bathroom, opening the frosted window, the better to enjoy the chorus of bird-song and the earthy scent of the bush while she brushed her teeth. Her mouth was full of foam when she heard the rumble of a high-performance engine floating up through the window. Was that the TVR in the driveway? She doubted Blake would be sneaking off to church!

She rinsed her mouth and gave her face a smear with a

dampened flannel, running her fingers through her wildly kinked hair as she hurried out to the stairs. She flew down the first flight, her bare feet silent on the thick carpet, and came to a skidding halt by the rail on the landing as she saw Blake with his back to her, one arm braced high against the open front door and security grille, greeting someone crossing the entry bridge. The back of his head was still bed-ruffled, he was barefoot, the belt of his black jeans dangling from the tabs at his hip, and—why hadn't he put on a shirt? His room was at the front corner of the house... He must have dashed down here as soon as he heard the car.

Nora crept forward for a better view, sidling up to a large ornamental urn stuffed with dried flowers so that she could see but not be seen.

The car was a late-model silver Mercedes convertible, the driver a *very* late-model blonde, her generous curves shrink-wrapped in a glittery pink crop-top and black leather mini-skirt. Her sequinned pink high-heeled sandals matched the wide leather belt that cinched her waist and her long straight hair was razor-cut to frame a youthful face boldly made up to seem older. From the way she was smiling as she stepped off the bridge on to the tiled porch she was supremely sure of her welcome. Was this one of Kate MacLeod's notorious twins?

'Hi, Blake.' The greeting was accompanied by a coy wiggle of coral-tipped fingers. Having got to the doorstep and finding that he wasn't stepping aside, the wattage of the smile increased. 'Surprise, surprise!' She placed her fingertips on Blake's chest and walked them provocatively up towards his unshaven chin. 'Happy to see me?'

Whoa!

Not very niecely behaviour, Nora fumed, watching Blake jerk his head back and catch the wandering fingers in his free hand.

'What are you doing here, Hayley?' His voice was neutral but Nora's straining ears detected a hint of deep unease.

The young woman gave a throaty laugh that made Nora revise her age up a few years. 'We had a date last night and you didn't show. It was a fantastic party, too; you really missed some fun.' She pouted a playful lower lip, slick with gloss, to show there were no hard feelings. 'I was *so* disappointed, but when Uncle Prescott explained all the pressure you were under and told me you'd snuck away for the weekend I realised that you just weren't in the party mood.'

Uncle Prescott? Nora's brain went on red alert. Hayley was the niece of Blake's boss? And she and Blake had been *dating*?

'Poor Blake,' Hayley was commiserating, snuggling up to his side with a nauseatingly kittenish air. 'Uncle Prescott said he was sure you didn't mean to let me down—you know how he likes to see me happy—so I decided to give you another chance. I thought I'd come and provide you with my special brand of stress relief....'

The kind of 'relief' she was talking about was obvious from the way her hand was creeping up Blake's thigh.

Nora's suspicions went ballistic. A red mist covered her vision and for a moment she thought she was going to be sick. For the first time she faced the real truth about her feelings for Blake. The dangerous attraction she had felt from the moment she first saw him wasn't just physical, but her painfully mixed up emotions had refused to believe she could have fallen for him so completely, so fast. Even when she had mistrusted his motives, she had still respected him and, yes, *admired* the fierce commitment he brought to everything, whether it be his lovemaking or his ruthless pursuit of his goals.

Only maybe his *real* goal was marrying the boss's niece!

At least this resolved any question of his paternity, she thought sickly. If Prescott Williams was keen on promoting a match between Blake and Hayley, then Blake couldn't be his son.

The red mist became a fog of fury. Kelly and Hayley—two spoilt young madams, both nieces of men who could pull company strings for their lovers!

Silently Nora fled back up the stairs and ducked into the first room she came upon—Blake's bedroom. Her wrathful gaze fell on the racks of clothes in the huge open wardrobe and her mouth curved in a vicious smile. She tore off her nightie and threw it on to the unmade bed. Naked but for her cotton briefs, she stormed over to the wardrobe and pulled a crisp white business shirt off its wooden hanger. She twisted it in savage fists and dragged the crumpled result on, rolling up the cuffed sleeves to her elbows and fastening five of the small pearlised buttons that marched down over her midriff. She looked at herself in the full-length mirror next to the bathroom door and undid the top button to reveal more cleavage. Leaning in to the mirror, she pinched roughly at her cheeks and chewed at her bottom lip. Her hair was sufficiently wild not to need any help in looking as if she had just climbed out of a passion pit!

Barely a couple of minutes had passed and when she reached the top of the stairs again she could hear the murmured conversation still going on at the door.

Let him talk himself out of *this*!

She took a deep breath that cleared some of the choking rage from her throat. Then she called out, using the sugar-sweet whine she had heard Kelly use when she wanted to twist a man around her manicured finger.

'Bla-ake! Where are you? Come on, Babycakes, what's taking you so long? You must have got rid of whoever it was by now!'

She heard the muted talk downstairs come to a sudden halt. 'Bla-ake! I'm getting cold and the champagne is getting warm!' she sang in a sexy lilt.

Dead silence. Nora began to trip down the stairs, changing her voice to a teasing sing-song. 'Oh, Bla-ake! Are we playing another of your kinky games of hide and seek? Then… coming, ready or no-ot!' she trilled, making the familiar playground call sound wickedly adult.

'Oh!' She came to a sudden stop halfway down the final

flight, one hand on the railing, the other covering her open mouth as she pretended to see the couple below for the first time. They were still standing in the doorway, Blake holding both of Hayley's hands in his.

'Oh, dear,' Nora gurgled. 'I didn't realise there was someone still here! I'm sorry, Blake. Have I let the cat out of the bag? I know we weren't supposed to let anyone know I was here....'

She waited expectantly for him to explode, but instead he appeared to be transfixed by shock as Hayley wrenched her hands out of his and said shrilly, 'Who's *she*? Why isn't anyone supposed to know? What's going on, Blake?'

'Yes, aren't you going to introduce us, Blake?' simpered Nora, slinking down the last few steps and sauntering up beside him.

'I don't think so,' he said with a tight-lipped grimness that gave her spiteful pleasure.

She mimicked Hayley's sulky pout and it must have been successful, for the younger girl took a step back, clutching her pink handbag to her glittering breasts, and sent Blake an angry look of scorching reproach.

'I'm Nora—Nora Lang,' said Nora helpfully, stirring the pot. 'Blake and I—well, we...' she ran a hand through her tousled curls, drawing attention to the suggestive pink marks on her cheeks and her sensuously bitten lips, as well as the brevity of her attire '...I suppose I *could* say we were just good friends, but in the circumstances that would be rather silly, wouldn't it?'

Hayley glared disdainfully at Nora with hard china-blue eyes, showing no hint of apology or discomfort.

'Uncle Prescott told me that you came down here *alone*,' she insisted stridently to Blake, wielding the name as an implied threat with such practised ease that Nora, who had been suffering a pang of empathy, felt her sympathy wither.

'Yes, well, "Uncle Prescott" isn't privy to everything that goes on in my personal life,' Blake replied coolly. 'Nowhere in my employment contract does it say that I have to clear it with the Chairman of the Board if I want to spend the weekend with the special woman in my life.'

Hayley's bee-stung mouth fell open and Nora sensed her own jaw sagging in stunned disbelief. She started to jerk away, experiencing a thrill of alarm, when Blake's arm snapped across her lower back, his heavy hand settling on her hip-bone, locking her against his hard flank. 'As I was saying before Nora so charmingly interrupted, you should have talked to me before driving all the way out here, Hayley. I could have saved you the trip.'

Hayley went pale with anger. 'You never seemed to mind me dropping in before!' she said petulantly, digging around in her handbag to produce a bright pink cell-phone. 'And anyway, I *did* call. I texted *and* left a message on your mobile to say I was coming, because every time I dialled it kept cutting straight to the answerphone!' She brandished the phone in his face.

'Perhaps the fact that I wasn't responding to my messages should have warned you that I didn't want to be disturbed.' Blake's cruel bluntness added to Nora's growing fear that she might have just made the biggest mistake of her life! 'I *have* asked you to stop turning up unannounced—to avoid just such an awkward situation as this,' he continued. 'I know that, as his late brother's stepchild, Scotty wants you and me to be friends, but even my family respects certain boundaries in my life. Naturally, I wouldn't have chosen to have you find out about Nora like this, but perhaps it's best that it's out in the open—'

'Then why did *she* say no one was supposed to know? You've never bothered to try and hide your mistresses before.' Hayley slashed wildly out at Nora. 'I suppose she's married or something!'

'Or something,' murmured Blake, his hand tightening warningly on Nora's hip as she stiffened. 'And Hayley—you and I *didn't* have a date last night. You told me last week that you were hosting a party on your uncle's yacht and invited me along. I said I'd see if I could make it. I didn't know then

what Nora was planning to do for the weekend. As you might
have gathered, I find her utterly irresistible and our time
together is precious…'

'*Blake!*' Nora was jolted out of her dumbstruck silence by
his outrageous embroidery, realising how thoroughly he had
turned the tables. Instead of trying to talk himself *out* of
trouble, he was intent on digging them in deeper, blatantly
using Nora as an excuse to extricate himself from the sticky
tentacles of an inconveniently possessive woman!

Before she could articulate her thoughts, he had pulled her
up on to her toes and kissed them out of her head with devastating efficiency. He hadn't yet shaved and the scrape of his
beard brought back torrid memories. By the time he let her
go her brain was so oxygen starved that black dots danced in
front of her eyes.

Through the mist of darkness she saw Hayley watching
them with a disturbingly malign intent. She still had the shiny
pink cell-phone clutched in her talons as she backed across the
porch.

'You won't care if I tell Uncle Prescott you're here with her
then!' she threatened, still refusing to dignify Nora with a name.

'That's up to you,' said Blake, relinquishing Nora to her
uncertain balance as he moved to see his unwelcome guest
on her way, 'but before you blow this trivial encounter out of
proportion, you might want to consider whether you want it
known that you intruded into my love-nest under the mistaken
impression that you'd be welcome. It might be less amusing
for your more bitchy friends if we can simply agree that this
never happened.'

Nora's last glimpse of Hayley was of a blonde fury flinging
herself into the convertible, a vindictive glitter of thwarted
rage in the sullen blue eyes.

Suddenly recalling that discretion was the better part of
valour, Nora felt silently for the tread with her bare toes as
she began to back stealthily up the stairs.

The security door clanged into place and the front door

swung closed with a definitive thud. Nora froze into wary stillness as Blake turned in a fluid ripple of muscle, his laser-like gaze zeroing in on her apprehensive face.

'I hope you're planning to iron that shirt when you've finished with it,' he said mildly.

'O-of course I will,' she stammered, smoothing the badly crumpled front, disconcerted by his calm. She would have been furious, *had* been furious, whenever he had questioned *her* honour.

'It *is* my shirt, isn't it?' he enquired, coming to stand at the bottom of the stairs, leaning a casual hip against the carving that decorated the end of the bannister rail.

She tensed. 'Um…yes, I—found it in your wardrobe….'

He didn't immediately demand to know what she had been doing rifling through his possessions. His inscrutable grey eyes dropped to her toes, curling to grip the stair carpet, then meandered slowly up her tense legs and over the creased white cotton to where the rumpled collar sagged to one side, almost sliding off her shoulder and revealing the small swell of one freckled breast.

'It suits you.'

'Oh!' Her eyes widened and she unconsciously clamped her thighs together to suppress the warm tingle that surged through her lower body at the unexpected compliment.

'Especially with nothing underneath…'

Uh-oh! Nora gulped as she remembered that this was one of Blake's masterly tactics—soften up your trembling victim with distracting trivialities and then pounce with tooth and claw when the guard drops. Best to try and get her explanations in first!

'Look, Blake, I'm sorry. I…I didn't mean—I overheard what was going on and I misunderstood—I—I just thought—'

'You thought I was an unscrupulous brute who'd callously seduce the boss's spoiled stepniece in order to feed my insatiable lust for money and power,' he said pleasantly.

'N-no—' Nora casually shifted her weight to disguise the tentative placement of her foot on the stair behind her.

'You were jealous,' he accused softly.

'*No!*' She instinctively protected her battle-scarred heart.

He straightened to his full height, half-naked…all man. 'Oh, yes—and so you decided to spike my guns by showing me up as a two-timing bastard with a secret taste for bold brassy tarts!'

He was still using that exquisitely calm voice, but Nora was no longer deceived. He was watching her like a hawk.

'FYI: Hayley and I have never been intimately involved,' he said quietly. 'She likes to play hostess for Scotty, but I stopped accepting invitations to social events with them when I realised that she was using them to persuade herself and others that we were a lot more than friends. I've been trying to discourage her without being offensive to her or to Scotty, but subtlety hasn't worked, and lately she's been verging on the obsessive.'

Conscious of his coiled tension, Nora hastened to repair the damage she had wrought. 'I—I lost my temper. I'm sorry. I hope it won't damage your relationship with Sir Prescott. If you like, I—I can go to him and explain—'

He stretched out his arm, placing his left hand flat on the bannister, parallel with the first step. 'Why don't you come down here and explain it to me first?' he invited with silky menace.

Nora licked her lips, her nerves stretched like piano wire, her breasts budding against the white cotton at the look in his eyes.

His nostrils flared, as if he had caught the alluring scent of her helpless excitement. He smiled.

'*Come on, Babycakes, what's taking you so long?*' he mocked.

Her nerve broke and she started to swivel on to her back foot. Her only warning was the green flash in his eyes a heart-beat before he exploded up the stairs, two at a time. She screamed and turned to run, managing to make three steps before she felt his fingers grab at her flying leg, slither down her calf and latch around her ankle. Clinging to the rail, she twisted her body and kicked out, all thoughts of modesty forgotten, and felt a connection with hard muscle, heard his curse, and was free to stumble up to the landing, where she dodged nimbly behind the tall stone-fired pottery urn.

Blake, hot on her heels, backhanded it casually out of the way and Nora gave another small scream as it crashed against the wall and spun around on the floor, spilling dried stalks across the small stretch of carpet between them.

They stared at each other across the debris, motionless, panting.

'You could have broken that,' Nora scolded piously.

His eyes flamed with unholy delight. 'Spank me!' He grinned and launched himself across the scattered flowers to snatch at the trailing edge of the white shirt.

Nora squeaked and skipped backwards, batting it out of his fingers. Seizing the bannister rail and whirling around, she vaulted herself up on to the next flight of stairs. They seemed to stretch for ever and Nora was already oxygen-depleted, her heart pumping furiously. Blake was stronger, but she was lighter and jet-powered by such a delicious terror that she managed to keep ahead of him for several breathless moments, until a mistimed step had her stumbling and this time when his hand clamped around her ankle, he wasn't letting go. His upward momentum carried his body up and over the back of hers, toppling her forward on to her knees, her hands still desperately clinging to the vertical rails supporting the bannister as he flattened her against the stairtreads and she felt in danger of becoming a human toboggan.

'Get off me, you oaf!' she gasped as the carpeted ridges bit into her squirming thighs.

'Hell-cat!' He let go her flailing ankle to grab her wriggling hips, his knees straddling hers, the heat of his heaving chest burning through the back of the shirt, the zip of his jeans pressing against her bottom. 'That's no way to talk to your lover!'

'Thug!' she said, trying to buck him off.

'Spitfire!' he groaned, and she realised the hardness against her bottom wasn't his metallic zip, it was what was behind it.

'Deviant!' she spat. 'Do you get turned on fighting helpless women?'

'Helpless? You nearly unmanned me with your kicks, you virago!'

'Well, I obviously didn't succeed, did I?' she said, pulling on the balusters to try and lever her body out from under him.

An insufferably arrogant chuckle fanned down the back of her neck as he merely caged her more closely with his arms and legs. 'If you wanted to turn me off you shouldn't have come prancing out in only my shirt, offering to play kinky games.'

'I said I was sorry—' she panted, the breath whooshing from her lungs. Somehow one of his hands had insinuated itself underneath her trapped body, sliding between the gaping buttons of the shirt and finding her breasts, suspended like firm, ripe fruit from her arched torso. He palmed each warm swaying mound in turn, thumbing the little stiff crests and enjoying her thready squeaks of unconvincing protest.

'Don't be sorry—this time you created exactly the right kind of trouble,' he murmured, rhythmically nudging her with his hips as his fingers trailed down to her quivering stomach to rim her belly button. 'I think this lesson in humility was just what Hayley needed to shock her out of her delusion that I'm hers for the asking—' He broke off as his fingers ran into an unexpected barrier.

'Well, well…not as wicked as you pretend to be, are you…?' He withdrew his hand to flip up the tail of the shirt and splay his hand over her exposed panties. 'Why, it's Mr Rabbit!' he exclaimed in deep tones of fond recognition, smoothing the printed cotton fabric over the plump curve of her blushing bottom. 'And look, there's a Mrs Rabbit, too, both primly dressed in their Sunday best. But bunnies are notorious for their lack of restraint. I wonder what naughtiness the pair of them get up to down here when the lights are out….' He stroked with his finger where Nora *knew* no bunnies frolicked, and she jerked violently.

'*Blake*…'

'Yes, Nora?' He leaned over her again, his mouth hot on the straining cords of her neck, the sharp prickle of his dark-blooming beard an exciting contrast to his warm wet tongue, his playful humour evaporating as his blind touch worked up under the band of elastic at the top of her thigh to slide against her creamy velvet centre. 'Oh, yes, you want me quite badly, don't you, Sparrow?'

She gave an incoherent choked cry that mingled with his hoarse sound of pleasure as he felt the slickness of her desire coat his fingers and explored the hot swollen folds of her womanhood where they curled protectively over the hidden kernel that had ripened into secret prominence.

'Sweet, sweet honey,' he murmured with impassioned reverence as he gently parted the petal-soft pleats of sensitised flesh between her legs, opening her moist heart to his exquisitely skilful and oh-so-delicate touch. 'Let it flow for me, baby…. Show me how sweet and hot and ready you are….' He nudged the tight little bud with the very tip of his finger and Nora felt it pulse with pleasure, sending a stream of sensation showering through her body, cascading over her breasts and belly and thighs like stinging sparks of incandescent fire.

Her spine arched, the rotation of her hips pushing her deeper back into the cup of his loins and he reacted violently to the invitation, dragging her panties roughly down her legs and tossing them carelessly over the bannister to flutter to the tiles below.

Nora felt the pressure of his denim-clad thighs suddenly ease on the back of her legs and heard a rustle and the rasp of a zip, the soft metallic hiss sending a flutter of apprehension beating along her singing veins.

She didn't want it to happen like this; she wanted to be able to *see* everything that he was feeling, to look into his eyes as he came into her, to touch him and fully participate in every glorious moment of anticipated bliss, not merely accepting, but loving, *sharing* in his mysterious male essence…

'Please—' She tried to twist an arm free and cried out

with pain when she banged an elbow against an overhanging tread.

'What's the matter?' He instantly shifted, rolling her over and frowning down into her watering eyes. His mouth twitched when she confessed that she had hit her funny bone.

'It's nothing to laugh at!' She practised her brand new pout. 'I'm probably going to have a lot of bruises later.'

His eyes darkened. 'I'm sorry; I'll kiss them better,' he said, lifting her slender arm and pressing his mouth to the tender curve of her elbow. His gaze fell to her bent legs. 'Every single one of them—wherever they might be,' he added gruffly, making her aware that he was lying propped between her splayed knees, and the bottom of the shirt had wiffled up around her waist. She blushed furiously and tried to push it down but he got there first.

'Here, let me help you with that.' He gripped the lower edges of the shirt and reared upwards, ripping them violently apart, scattering buttons in all directions, leaving Nora quivering with delicious shock and quite forgetting her physical discomfort.

'That's better!' he announced with raw satisfaction as he studied her blush-pink and cinnamon-speckled nudity draped over the stairs, lingering longest on the downy triangle of autumn-brown curls which sheltered the treasure he had already begun to plunder.

Nora felt as if she was burning up under his fiery inspection, her limbs too heavy with molten desire to rise in defence of her modesty, fascinated by the ragged rise and fall of his deep chest and the compact ripple of his flat abdomen where it arrowed into the open fly of his unzipped jeans. Wanton curiosity led her to discover that his tan *did* go all the way, disappearing into the bold black thicket of hair that filled out the base of the 'V'.

'You're not wearing anything under your jeans,' she blurted, and he looked down at himself, indecently amused by her prudish surprise. This, from a sexy sparrow without the remaining wisp of a feather to fly with!

'Shortly to be remedied!' he murmured with a shameless smile, reaching into his back pocket to produce a slim wallet, from which he extracted a small familiar-looking package.

Bracing himself on one arm, he leaned forward until the ends of his loosened belt brushed her inner thighs, the cold kiss of the buckle making her skin jump. He dipped his head to place a kiss between her tip-tilted breasts, at the same time placing the feather-light gift in her hand. She blinked at it uncomprehendingly and he urged softly, 'I want you to put it on me….'

Her eyes widened. 'Oh! But I— Sh-shouldn't we wait until we get into the bedroom?'

'Not when we're going to need it right here. Right now,' he advised her with hoarse intensity, letting her feel the fine tremors of barely leashed tension that racked his body, his hand silking over the hollow of her hip to toy pointedly with one of her dewy-damp curls.

Make love on the stairs? How outrageous, how reckless, how daring! How very un-Nora! Her eyes skittered down to the blatant invitation of his open jeans, and up again. Incurably honest, she had to try, 'I'm not very…' She tailed off, thinking better of mentioning that Ryan had always been in too much of a hurry to waste time with her inept fumbling! 'I— It may take me a bit longer than you're used to, to put it on,' she confessed awkwardly.

'Oh, really?' His eyelids drooped, turning his eyes into glittering slits of smouldering approval. 'You promise?'

Her flustered response gave him licence to torment her with more sizzling suggestions. 'I'll help you, then, shall I? It might even take longer that way….'

And with that he threaded his fingers around the back of her head and slanted his open mouth fiercely across hers, flooding her with the rich taste and scent of aroused male, inciting her to new levels of excitement with low, throaty sounds of carnal hunger. The insecurity of their awkward, slanting position and the odd protrusions and difficult angles only heightened the erotic intensity, emphasising the vora-

ciousness of their need. Nora gloried in the textures of his turbulent loving—the prickly roughness of his jaw, the silkiness
of his tongue, the oiled sweep of his muscles, the feathery
stroke of his hair. Caught up in the passion of the moment,
she was hardly aware of him picking up her empty hand until
he forced it down into his open jeans, moulding her fingers
around the thick shaft that tucked down one leg, tenting the
heavy fabric. Nora gasped as she touched the swollen
hardness she had secretly fantasised about—hot and smooth
as satin-wrapped steel, yet pulsating with life, with the
promise of eternity, of *new* life…

He gave a clotted moan of pleasure as her fingers fluttered
curiously down to find the lightly lubricated tip, trapped
against his thigh by the cut of his jeans, measuring his full
length as more than the span of her hand. His grip on her wrist
tightened involuntarily, his hips thrusting to increase the
friction of her palm, and he groaned.

'That's right, Sparrow… Now take me out,' he begged
roughly, and it was Blake, the expert, who was fumbling as
he guided her to free his swollen flesh from the prison of
denim and sheath him in the snug new covering. True to her
warning, she was not very deft, afraid of hurting him and a
little awed by his size. She handled him with gentle care,
until the prince of sexual self-mastery was sweating and
shaking and gritting his teeth to stop himself coming like
an inexperienced schoolboy before she even had the damned
thing halfway on! It didn't help him that he could see she
was just as aroused herself, her rosy breasts tight and
swollen as they dipped and swayed, the pert nipples
yearning for his mouth.

'That's enough,' he shuddered at last, pushing her hands
away and kicking off the confining jeans so that he could
scoop her bottom to the edge of the stair and drive gratify-
ingly deep at his first thrust.

Nora was seduced, invaded, conquered and won in that first
instant of possession. The blunt force of his entry was almost

painful, but it was a sweet, savage, soul-satisfying pain that she sought again and again, the liquid heat of her body quickly adjusting to his daunting size, accepting him, welcoming him, drawing him deeper with tiny rhythmic convulsions of muscle which resonated in every nerve and cell of her being. His face was tight, his expression tense with concentration, his grey eyes intent on reading the unspoken signals that told him of her intoxicating enthusiasm for his every move.

Her rapturous response unleashed an insatiable demand, his increasingly urgent thrusts lifting her body, driving her sideways with every cycle of surge and retreat until her back was jammed against the balusters, the small of her back riding the ridge of a stair. Her hands slipped on his perspiration-slick shoulders and she anchored herself by wrapping her arms around him, splaying her fingers over the thrilling bunch and flex of his long back, trying to relieve the pressure on her back by twining her supple legs around his plunging hips.

He must have seen the gathering cloud in her golden eyes for suddenly he gave a convulsive heave and the world was awhirl and when she recovered her equilibrium she found herself on top of him, seated astride his lap as his broad back took the brunt of their combined weight against the stairs, his legs drawn up behind her back, providing her with extra support. Startled, she began to push up on to her knees, but he caught her hips and re-seated her with a jolting thrust.

'Don't leave me,' he ground out, the earthy plea paralysing her heart, making her faint with wild and foolish hopes.

'I don't want to hurt you—' she whispered shakily, leaning her hands against the stair on either side of his straining shoulders to try and redistribute the load on his back, conscious of him pressing up against the entrance of her womb, stunned by the ravishing feel of all that unrestrained power riding between her thighs.

'The only way you can hurt me now is if you stop,' he gritted, rocking his hips to tilt her further forward so that he could reach her breasts with his mouth. Stretching out to eagerly cooperate with his wordless demand, Nora watched the sides of the shirt billow out around his head, enclosing them in an erotic haven of filtered light, thickly perfumed with mutual desire. Thick pulses of liquefied pleasure spurted between her legs as she watched him lapping at her painfully distended nipples with his skilful tongue before drawing them fully into his hot mouth to suckle hungrily.

The end, when it came, was sublimely shattering, yet even that was infused with his unique blend of passion and devilry. As her hips began to churn and Blake's body to quake with uncontrollable spasms he tore his mouth from her breasts and threw back his head to meet her tempest-tossed gaze.

'Coming, ready or not...' he rasped with impeccable timing, and Nora's explosion of violent delight was intensified by paroxysms of helpless laughter. Which made it all the more inexplicable when, sprawling full length in his arms, weak with exhausted pleasure, she surprised them both by bursting into raw tears, sobbing into his heaving chest.

Gentle hands stroked and soothed up and down her shaking back while she apologised, shuddering hiccups causing interesting sensations in their still-joined bodies as she sought to explain away her foolish tears without embarrassing either of them with rash declarations of love, and spoiling what should be a perfect moment of post-coital bliss. Of course, a sophisticated lover like Blake would be appalled at all this excess emotion. He might even begin to fear that he had another potential stalker on his hands....

She fished beside him for the shirt which had been wrenched off in the throes of their final climactic eruption and dragged it to hide her face and blot her tears.

'It was my first time on top,' she said inconsequentially, sniffing into the crumpled folds.

The hand patting her back stilled. 'And it was so awful it made you cry?'

She wrenched the shirt away from her dismayed face,

causing him to utter a stifled groan as she dislodged him by squirming to sit up and impress him with her earnest reassurances. 'No! Oh, *no*—it was *beautiful*!' she said. 'It's just... Oh, I don't *know* why—'

'I would think it was obvious,' he said kindly. 'I've just given you the most spectacular orgasm of your life, and now you've realised what you've been missing out on all these years.'

'Why you arrogant—!' Realising he was teasing to help banish her hectic embarrassment, Nora broke off and tried to stuff his shirt into his laughing mouth. Thank God he didn't know how close to the truth he was!

He sprang up and chased her, shrieking, up to the top of the stairs, where he snatched her up and carried her ceremoniously to his big bed, tumbling them both down on to the unmade sheets.

'Now that I've finally got you where you belong, I think there's something you should know about me,' he said, pinning her to the luxurious mattress with a warm hairy thigh.

She ran her hands over his rough jaw, exulting in her new freedom to touch. There were other ways to express love. It didn't have to be in words.

'What should I know?'

He bent and nipped at her shoulder. 'That I really am an unscrupulous brute with an insatiable appetite...for *you*.'

CHAPTER ELEVEN

As LOVE-LETTERS went it was a fairly pathetic effort:

> *Nora,*
> *Sorry, but I had to do it this way.*
> *Have arranged for someone to collect you.*
> *Call you later.*
> *Blake*

God forbid that he should have signed 'love, Blake' after they had just spent two whole passion-saturated days—and nights—making love with each other, Nora thought wistfully. She apparently hadn't even ranked a 'Best wishes' or 'Kind regards', although in the circumstances a 'Yours faithfully' would have been nice!

He had been insatiable in more ways than one—an exciting, witty, wonderful companion, flatteringly interested in her thoughts and opinions and free with his own. He had shown her that laughter and fun could be an integral part of lovemaking and had showered her with words of passion and praise, and even tenderness, but he had been scrupulously honest. He had made no reckless promises.

Still, at least he had cared enough to leave a note, rather than just abandoning her while he raced off to oversee his all-important stock market bid. And he *had* lingered until after

dawn to bring her breakfast in bed…a breakfast which he had
proceeded to share with an ardent enthusiasm that had left his
sheets gritty with toast crumbs and sticky with honey. It was
while Nora was showering off her syrupy body and donning
Friday's blouse and skirt in expectation of having to scurry
to work as soon as they arrived back in Auckland, that Blake
had made his discreet exit.

Call you later? How reassuring! How *vague*. Was she just
supposed to hang around at home waiting for him to bother
to contact her? And what about his cavalier attitude to her job?

Turning over the square of expensive paper and finding the
security alarm code scrawled on the back, Nora wondered if
she was supposed to feel gratified by this example of his
trust. His faith in her seemed to be sadly limited to trivialities. He would trust her with his beach house, but not with
his honour? She wanted, no, she *deserved*, far more from him
than that! She wasn't going to let him assume that she could
be packed tidily away in a convenient box until he was ready
to take her out and play with her again!

Unfortunately, her search for a telephone proved fruitless—thanks, she was sure, to the one room he had kept
locked. But when she went down to look through the garage
she had been surprised to see the TVR still parked in its spot.
For some reason Blake had taken the four-wheel drive back
to town rather than his beloved sports car. A wicked little light
went on in Nora's brain. A further, more detailed, search of
his bedroom turned up the car's electronic key and after some
experimentation she managed to unlock the doors and boot
without setting off the alarm.

Carrying her laptop back upstairs, she plugged it into the
supposedly unconnected phone line and powered up to the
site of a broadband link to an ISP who also happened to be
her own. She wouldn't even have to re-configure her modem!

'Hah! I knew you were lying,' she crowed, tapping at the
keyboard. First item on the agenda: an Internet phone call to
her boss at Maitlands.

Half an hour later her hands were slipping sweatily on the steering wheel of the TVR as she finally jerked out of the gravelled side road and on to the Waitakere dual carriageway. There had been no manufacturer's booklet in the car but after she had downloaded the results of her Internet search on the Cerbera she thought she had all the information she needed.

She now knew why Blake had chosen not to drive it back to Auckland. From the noises it was making there was something seriously wrong…unless it was just her driving. For a ghastly moment Nora wondered if she'd crept all the way up the steep gradient with the handbrake on. She glanced down to check and in doing so must have turned the wheel, for the steering reacted with the quickness for which it had been fashioned and the car headed obediently into the clay ditch at the side of the road.

With a graunching of its low-slung rear, the TVR settled at a drunken angle in the shallow depression. Quickly Nora punched the red button under the steering wheel and there was instant silence from the engine. She closed her eyes in stricken disbelief.

She didn't know how long she sat there, her head bowed over the steering wheel, but she was roused from her misery by a tap on the window. A car had stopped on the opposite side of the road and a tall dark-haired woman had crossed over to bend down and peer in at Nora's wilting figure. Nora searched for the little button on the side pocket which opened the door and climbed gingerly out.

'Are you OK?' The woman looked to be in her mid-thirties, wearing mirrored sunglasses and a smart suit which made Nora feel drab.

'Fine.' She smiled shakily. 'I don't think the car is, though.'

To her outraged astonishment the woman started laughing when she walked around to study the rear of the car. 'I'm afraid not! Boy, is he ever going to be ticked!'

She came sauntering back, removing her sunglasses and Nora found herself staring up into a pair of very familiar-looking grey eyes.

'On the other hand, it could just strengthen your hand if you want to make a personal grievance claim.' The woman's eyebrows snapped together thoughtfully as she tapped her folded sunglasses against her mouth. 'You do know you could sue him for what he's done? You could make megabucks if he detained you without your consent—and then there's the question of restraint of trade...I mean, his actions prevented you from working at your job, right?'

'Right! You must be Maria,' Nora said drily, recognising more than a superficial family resemblance.

'How did you guess?' The older woman grinned, arching her thick black eyebrows. 'And you're Nora. I just know we're going to get on like a house on fire.'

'I think I've caused enough damage for one day without adding arson to the list,' Nora said glumly. 'Did Blake send you to give me a lift home?'

'Hell, no!' Maria looked swiftly around as if her brother might rampage out from the bushes. 'He'd have a fit if he knew I knew! No, I just happened to be at Mum's when he rang and asked her to do him a favour. He gave her a quick run-down on the situation—' she laughed at Nora's appalled face '—expurgated, I'm sure!' She turned and waved at the other car and Nora saw a slim grey-haired version of the woman beside her waving back.

'He asked his *mother* to come and get me?' she squeaked.

'Yeah, I guess you don't know yet what a terrible Mamma's boy he is! He didn't mention that you might be using his TVR, though.' She looked at Nora's guilt-stricken face and skated briskly on. 'Anyway, let's transfer your stuff and lock up. I'll make a call to Blake's mechanic and we can leave this heap of expensive junk for the tow-truck to pick up.'

Nora wasn't sure what to say to her lover's mother, but Mrs MacLeod soon solved the problem. She directed her daughter to take the wheel and joined Nora in the back seat, getting down to brass tacks by dismissing Nora's garbled attempts to tell her about the car as irrelevant to the key issue. 'So…how do you feel about my son?'

At least her eyes weren't that haunting grey that sent shivers up Nora's spine. They were a very kindly, but very insistent blue. 'I— We only met last Thursday—'

'That wasn't what I asked.' Pamela MacLeod smiled. In jeans and a sweatshirt, she didn't look very intimidating, but Nora had a feeling that tenacity was another common family trait.

'I…well—' God, how did you describe a man who was great in bed to his *mother*? With his sister listening? Nora could feel herself pinken. 'He's very—very um—'

'Interesting?'

That would work! 'Yes, Mrs MacLeod, he's very interesting.'

'Call me Pam.' The grey head tilted enquiringly. 'In what way would you say he was interesting?'

Nora began to sweat. 'Well, he's a… He's very complex…. He has a very…er…forceful personality….'

'Yes, he's very like his father in that respect,' said his forceful mother. 'No looks or charm to speak of, so he has to make up for it in charisma!'

What planet was this woman living on? 'Blake's an extremely attractive man!' contested Nora hotly.

'Oh, I didn't say he wasn't *attractive*,' Pam replied with a twinkling smile that softened her angular face into maternal smugness. 'Just that he's not pretty in that metrosexual way that's so popular these days. His father was a big, gruff, crude man—but I like a bit of the primitive in a man, don't you?'

Nora wasn't going to touch that one with a ten-foot pole. 'His father?' she stumbled. 'You mean your husband?'

'Yes. Neil. Who else would I mean?' Unfortunately Blake's mother was as alarmingly perceptive as her son. 'Don't tell me you've heard that silly story about *Prescott*.' She looked amused. 'Have you ever *met* Prescott Williams?'

Nora tried to ignore the snickers floating over from the driver's seat. 'No.'

'Well, let me put it this way. If I'd ever been tempted to

cheat on my Neil, it wouldn't have been with a skinny runt he could have picked up with his little finger! Now—' She settled more comfortably in her seat, her sharp eyes on Nora's embarrassed face. 'Blake tells me he whisked you away without so much as a by-your-leave this weekend, but he didn't really explain why.... Just some nonsense about you getting tangled up in some deal he was doing. What line of work are you in, Nora?'

Nora was a limp dish-rag by the time the two women dropped her off on the front steps of her apartment building, wrung dry of explanations, excuses, evasions and her personal history from the year dot.

'Thanks for the lift Maria, Mrs—er, Pam,' she croaked, searching out her spare door key while his mother held her laptop.

'You can thank Blake,' said Pam. 'I was just his stand-in. He seemed very anxious that you didn't get the impression that he was trying to get rid of you by fobbing you off on some paid minion.'

Nora, who had thought that very thing, smiled weakly.

'He also told me I wasn't to put you on the spot by asking any embarrassing questions about the two of you,' admitted Pam, without a flicker of shame. 'So, perhaps you'd like to leave it to me to tell Blake about his car getting a tiny scuff?' she continued, blatantly indulging in a little friendly black-mail. 'These things are much better coming from one's mother. I shall make sure he knows that it's all his own fault for acting like a caveman in the first place. If he had any social conscience he wouldn't be driving such a glaring symbol of conspicuous consumption, anyway!'

Nora was spinelessly quick to accept the quid pro quo, and for the rest of the day she grinned whenever she thought of Blake being scolded by his mother into accepting the blame for the accident.

She found precious little else to smile about. Kelly had definitely moved out some time over the weekend, taking not only all of her own things, but several of Nora's as well, leaving a pile of unwanted junk strewn in her wake. Having already made the phone call from the beach house to let her boss know that she would back to work by the afternoon, Nora turned her back on the mess and drove to the office, where she conscientiously tried to compress everything she should have done on Friday into half a day's schedule. It didn't take her long to find out that Kelly had moved into Ryan's apartment on Saturday and that she was now flashing a brand-new diamond ring on her engagement finger. Nora was proud of herself when she came unexpectedly face-to-face with Ryan in the coffee room and cheerfully congratulated him on finding his perfect match, adding in dulcet tones that Kelly could keep the set of crystal wineglasses she had taken, as an engagement present.

At one stage she did peek at the on-line financial news and was unsurprised to see that the headliner was PresCorp's successful stand in the market for TranStar shares. Had Blake ever failed at what he set out to do? PresCorp had apparently reached its targeted holding within minutes of the start of morning trading. So her exciting career as a suspected *femme fatale* was officially over, Nora thought wryly as she logged off.

Then, when she answered her cell-phone not recognising the caller's number, she got a delicious shock.

'What in the hell are you doing in at work?' a voice snarled in her ear.

'And good afternoon to you too, sir!' replied Nora briskly, all too aware of the drawbacks of working in an open-plan office.

'My mother said you refused to let her call an ambulance, or take you to the A&E clinic to get you checked out.' Blake had no time to waste on pleasantries. 'She said she thought you could have delayed concussion—'

Nora closed her eyes. He sounded furious. 'Uh...your car—'

'To hell with the car!' he swore. 'Are *you* all right? Mum

said you were as white as a ghost and she thought you were limping….'

To hell with his car? Oh, thank you, thank you, Mrs MacLeod! Nora took a deep breath. 'I'm fine, really, it was nothing—!'

'If it was nothing then why does your voice sound so weak and wobbly?' he snapped suspiciously.

Because she was trying not to laugh. She cleared her throat. 'Look, can we talk about this later? I'm not supposed to accept personal calls at work and my boss is glaring at me.'

She paid for her insouciance later that evening when Blake coolly let himself into her flat with her keys and made very short work of extracting a full and frank confession.

'I swear it wasn't deliberate, Blake,' Nora gasped apologetically, as he finally completed his very thorough, and ferociously intimate, inspection of her body. 'It was just a lot harder to handle than I thought it would be when I started out….'

'I know the feeling,' he muttered, rolling off her and collapsing on his back, taking up most of her narrow single bed. 'I should have known it was dangerous to leave you on your own. And then to toss Mum into the mix—I should have realised you'd gang up on me!'

Nora almost felt sorry for him. Almost. 'I'd offer to pay for the damage but your sister said I shouldn't admit any liability,' she teased huskily.

'It was going in for an overhaul, anyway. I didn't like the sound of it when I turned over the engine this— Wait! Liability? Maria! *Maria* was there, too?' He raised his head to scowl at her. 'Damn it! I told Mum this was to be kept *low-key*—'

Nora felt a freezing touch kill the delicate tendril of hope that had begun to unfurl in her breast. She scolded herself for her naivety and maintained her warm tone of amusement. 'Maria said I should sue you for restraint of trade.'

His frown turned into a sexy grin as he took her back in his arms. 'Make it *lack* of restraint and I might be willing to deal!'

If Nora thought it was challenging to try and maintain a 'low-key' affair with a dynamic and powerful man, by the beginning of the following week she was faced with the far more difficult prospect of living in a high-profile scandal.

'But you can't fire me; I haven't done anything wrong!' she protested to her boss.

'You're not being fired, just suspended,' Ruben Jensen said uncomfortably. 'Sorry, Eleanor, I'm just following orders. The Acquisitions and Takeovers people are in a flap and TranStar's chairman is screaming dirty tricks to the Market Surveillance Panel. You must admit this doesn't create a very good impression.' His lined face looked harassed as he tapped the tabloid which had hit the news-stands the previous day.

Nora snatched it up, glaring at the two photographs of the half-clad couple under the splashy headline. In the larger picture the woman locked in Blake MacLeod's embrace in the doorway of his beach house could have been anyone, but the smaller inset showed the moment the kiss had broken off and Nora's back was no longer to the camera, her face clearly identifiable. No, not camera, she thought furiously—*cell-phone*. The furious Hayley had had the last word after all. She must have taken the photos with her phone, and now the PXTs were in the public arena.

Nora scanned the copy with rising ire. The story was heavy on conjecture and light on facts, concerned mainly with drooling over Blake's reputed past bedding of several celebrities and how close-mouthed he generally was about his affairs. But it did identify Nora by name—oh, why had she foolishly introduced herself to Hayley?—and a little journalistic rummaging had mis-identified her as a stock analyst for Maitlands and threw up the connection between the company she worked for and TranStar.

'This is all total rubbish!' she declared, flinging it back down on Ruben's desk.

'Yes, well, unfortunately one of our employees brought it to the notice of management and all hell has broken loose,' he said. 'And someone has confirmed that you and MacLeod *did* spend that weekend away together, including the Friday you were supposedly home sick...'

Nora's heart plummeted. Kelly! Or Ryan. Or both of them. She, who had never made an enemy before, suddenly seemed to be besieged with influential foes!

'But they're saying I might have passed on inside information! That's just ridiculous—I didn't know anything about the takeover to pass on,' Nora cried.

'I know, but with your security clearance you have access to a lot of sensitive stuff, and maybe you didn't even realise what he was doing. You know, you're way too trusting, Nora. Do you really think he's just interested in *you*...?' Ruben probably thought he was being supportive; he didn't even realise how insulting he was being, to Nora as well as to Blake.

'Don't I get a hearing first? What if I refuse to accept this suspension?' she said angrily.

But no amount of argument could budge her boss.

'Nora, under the terms of your contract, I'm afraid you don't have a choice.' Ruben was beginning to looked alarmed by her unaccustomed fierceness. 'If you'll hand in your key-card and your laptop, I'll get a member of the security staff to escort you out.'

A short time later Nora stood in front of the towering PresCorp building on the fringe of the city's wharf district, buffeted by a stream of lunch-time workers exiting the building. She had not only burnt her bridges, she feared she had set fire to her entire transport system with her explosion of outrage.

She shouldered her capacious bag—the one which had been searched by security before she left Maitlands—and stalked across the marble foyer to the information desk.

'Where do I find Mr MacLeod's office?' she asked the bored-looking man who was signing for a delivery.

'Executive suite's on the seventeenth floor,' he informed her, without looking up from the clipboard. 'Take the lift over there to the tenth-floor lobby, turn left and follow the signs. The executive lift will take you the rest of the way.'

Nora was so busy stewing over what she was going to say if and when she got in to see Blake, that it was only as she was stepping out on the seventeenth floor that she realised that 'executive lift' had been a euphemism for one of the fashionable glass-sided monstrosities, and that she had ridden up looking out over the city without even registering the fact. Smoothing down her navy skirt and making sure her fuchsia blouse was tucked in, she approached the executive receptionist, who exhibited the polished sympathy of a hardened professional as she listened to Nora's request for a personal meeting with the most sought after man in the building.

She obviously didn't read the tabloids because, before Nora had even finished speaking, she launched into her stonewalling routine.

'Hi, there! Here to see Blake?'

Nora turned and for a moment didn't connect the smooth-faced young man in the Hugo Boss suit with the bristly, bronzed surfer.

'Oh, hello, Steve. Have you started your internship already? That was fast work.'

He grinned. 'I got suspended from school for smoking and persuaded Blake to take me on early. You might say we exchanged favours. He rang me down at the beach last Tuesday afternoon, foaming at the mouth about his TVR being in a ditch somewhere up in the hills and asking me if I would ride back to town with the mechanic to make sure he didn't treat her too harshly.'

Nora blushed. 'Oh, dear. Did he say how it happened?'

'Funny thing, he never did. He was as touchy as hell about it!' Steve gave her a familiar wink that suggested he knew more than he was telling. He was *definitely* a tabloid reader! 'Hey, you want me to take you along to his office?'

The receptionist intervened with stern talk of back-to-back appointments, but the upshot of his friendly interference was that she eventually conducted Nora into a spacious office with a huge picture window that looked out over the glittering Waitemata Harbour.

Her stomach lurched, not at the sight of the bobbing ferries docked far below, but at the wizened sprite of a man with a thick shock of white hair who was seated behind the huge wooden desk in front of the window. A man whose portrait hung prominently in the waiting area.

'I think there must be some mistake—' She started backing out.

'No, no!' Sir Prescott Williams leapt to his feet. 'When Sandra said you were waiting for Blake I told her to bring you in here. Wanted to meet you.' He limped around the desk, his dark suit jacket flapping open, and seized Nora's hand, shaking it with a vigour that made her teeth rattle. 'Prescott Williams—you can call me Scotty—Blake always does. It's Nora, isn't it?'

'Yes, but—'

'Sit down! Sit down!' He led her over to a buttoned leather couch and urged her into it, standing over her, rocking on his heels, brows beetling over his black-button eyes. 'I can get Sandra to bring some tea, if you like. Or what do you say we both have a *real* drink? Sun well over the yard-arm and all that!' He sprang across the room and whipped open a bulging drinks cabinet, rubbing his hands together as he looked over his shoulder at her. 'Join me in a whisky? Or do you prefer that rot-gut vodka that Blake drinks?' He spun around, his face creasing with sudden inspiration. 'Or we could open a bottle of champagne—make a proper toast.'

The thought of vodka made Nora feel green, and why she would want to toast the smoking ruins of her career and reputation was beyond her. She decided to try to assert some ownership of the situation. 'Sir Prescott, I don't know what you've read in the papers, but—'

'Oh, no need to worry about the *papers*.' He waved a knobbly blue-veined hand in contempt. 'Blake has all that well in hand. Told me the whole story. Silly girl Hayley got the wrong end of the stick! Typical—not the sharpest tool in the box! Whisky, was it you said you wanted?' He clinked the glass hopefully and Nora knew that if she didn't say yes he would gallantly refuse to have one himself.

She agreed, dying to ask exactly what story he had been told to make him sound so cheerfully unconcerned.

He limped across with the glasses and plonked himself down on the couch beside her, extending his leg in front of him. 'Damned hip—they tell me I have to have a new one put in next month. Cheers!' He clinked his glass against hers. 'Drink up! Drink up!'

Nora sipped cautiously and coughed politely into her hand, blinking rapidly to try and clear the tears in her eyes.

Sir Prescott chuckled. 'That'll put hair on your chest!' He settled back, black eyes snapping. 'Work for Maitlands, do you? Computers and all that rigmarole. Pity!'

Nora wasn't quite sure what she was being pitied for, so she took another sip of her whisky, which encouraged her to admit bravely, 'I don't…work at Maitlands any more, I mean. I quit. Today.'

The black eyes lit up. 'Good! Good! Blake persuaded you to come to us, has he? Cunning lad. Says you're a top brain. Talked you up a storm. Mentioned that you're working on something of your own that could be just up our alley…software for use in sea-bed salvage work.' He took a long, satisfied gulp of his drink, not noticing Nora's stunned expression. 'That's how I started this little empire of mine, you know— in the marine salvage business.' He chuckled. 'That programme of yours sounds as if it might have uses in the underwater construction and drilling fields, too. Maybe you should be thinking of getting some investment capital behind you to help develop your ideas and diversify them into commercial applications. And if it's finance you're after, well, I'm always on the lookout to invest in up-and-comers with bright ideas. Of course, if we negotiated our way into doing some business together, that would be over and above any salary you make with PresCorp….'

Nora lubricated her frozen vocal cords with a warm trickle of whisky. 'Sir—uh…Scotty, I haven't really even thought about—'

Suddenly the door crashed open and Blake strode into the room with a thunderous scowl. 'What the devil is going on?'

'Ah, there you are, boy. We were wondering where you'd got to, weren't we, Nora?' Sir Prescott said blandly.

Blake's eyes took on a strange glitter as they whipped suspiciously back and forth between the pair on the couch. 'Were you? How strange, then, that Sandra never bothered to tell me that Nora was here to see me. I had to learn it from some pimply intern.' He prowled over to frown at the older man. 'I thought the doctor had told you to cut down on the hard stuff until after your operation?'

Sir Prescott's bony knuckles whitened on his glass, as if he was afraid Blake would snatch it away. 'This is a special occasion.'

'Yes, Scotty was just offering to back me in a business venture,' said Nora, nervously defiant. 'Apparently you've been telling him all about the sea-bed project I'm working on—'

'*Scotty?*' Blake folded his arms across his chest as he loomed over her, looking magnificently menacing in his black suit, black silk shirt and steel-grey tie. 'I had no idea you two were such friends.'

'Come off it, Blake. I may have jumped the gun but I thought this was what you wanted.' Sir Prescott chuckled at his stony expression. 'It was your idea to offer this clever fiancée of yours a job. And, lucky for us, she says she's already quit the other mob—'

Fiancée? Nora scooted forward on the couch. 'Oh, but we're n—'

Blake abruptly shifted his stance, a black-clad knee

bumping her arm, upending her whisky glass in her lap. She jumped to her feet with a shriek, brushing at the sodden linen, which had sucked up the liquid like a thirsty alcoholic and now clung drunkenly to her legs.

'What a waste of good Scotch,' mourned Sir Prescott, picking up her empty glass.

'I don't think it'll stain if you rinse it out immediately,' murmured Blake and Nora froze as she recognised the words she had said to him on the first night they met. He took her elbow, propelling her to the door, barely giving her time to grab her bag. 'Come on, you can use the bathroom in my private office.'

'Good idea. Can't have you going round smelling like a distillery,' chipped in Sir Prescott helpfully, limping after them. 'Tell you what—you go off with Blake and get cleaned up and I'll round everyone up and open a few bottles of that champagne so we can properly toast your engagement when you come back. I'll get Sandra to send out for some food, too, shall I, Blake? May as well go the whole hog. Perhaps even a cake—'

'*You!*—' Blake halted his Chairman with a disrespectful finger poked into his chest '—have done enough. Thank you, but I'll take this from here.'

He slammed the door on Sir Prescott's expression of injured innocence and hustled Nora back through the reception area, scowling at anyone who dared approach.

'Why did you do that? What was he *talking* about?' Nora burst out when she had been frogmarched into a luxurious blue and grey office which mirrored the layout of the one they had just left. 'Oh, for God's sake, don't bother,' she said impatiently, as he picked up the remote control from the desk to close the vertical blinds. 'If I came up in that wretched glass box of yours without turning a hair, I'm hardly going to keel over now! I want to know what you've been saying to Sir Prescott, and why he thinks we're engaged!'

'Did you?' He dropped the remote and spun around to study her.

'Did I what?' she asked distractedly, wrinkling her dainty nose as she lifted the saturated skirt away from her damp tights.

'Handle the lift without panicking?'

She shrugged, trying not to be disarmed by the warmth of encouragement in his eyes. 'I had other things on my mind,' she said.

'Like quitting your job? You've really left Maitlands?' He slipped off his jacket and hung it over the back of his chair.

'They tried to suspend me, so I told my boss he could make it my period of notice,' Nora said, her temper flaring all over again as she described the encounter. 'Ruben was even talking about honey traps—'

'Mmm, well, I do seem to recall at least *one* occasion when honey did feature rather prominently in our relationship,' said Blake with unblushing calm. 'Otherwise their investigation is going to be a waste of their time and money. Now, why don't you take your skirt off and I'll get my secretary to send it out to the one-hour laundry service. That wet patch is far too big to try and blot with a towel—'

'And whose fault is that? What on earth am I supposed to do in here without a skirt for an hour?' she snapped unthinkingly, and went the same colour as her blouse as he started laughing. 'Damn it, Blake—'

'I'm sorry, Sparrow, I can't help it—I love seeing you with ruffled plumage.'

Still laughing, he fetched a long black towelling robe from the adjacent bathroom and, flustered by the rare endearment and by his casual use of the 'L' word, Nora put it on, wriggling out of her skirt under his amused eye and stripping off her tights to drape over the bathroom rail while he spoke to his middle-aged secretary. When his poker-faced employee had left, he remained leaning against the closed door, looking at Nora as she nervously tightened the belt of the bulky robe.

'I'm sorry about your job,' he said gravely. 'But I was serious about wanting to offer you one here. PresCorp has a big IT department and they're always aggressively head-hunting for experienced staff of your calibre. I also regret I didn't handle the problem of Hayley earlier, and protect you better from the inevitable fallout when our relationship went public…'

'I don't think I was going to stay on at Maitlands anyway,' she admitted with a sigh. 'It would have been too awkward. Ryan and Kelly have just got engaged—' She broke off, suddenly remembering the reason she had been given a whisky bath. 'Why did you want to stop me talking to Sir Prescott?' She tensed in alarm as she foresaw a potentially cringe-making scene. 'He wasn't serious, was he, about getting everyone in for a champagne toast to our engagement?'

Blake's shoulders lifted under the black silk. 'Unfortunately, when Scotty gets his mind fixed on something it's well nigh impossible to change it. He's ferociously stubborn and a rampant opportunist—'

'Gee, now who does that sound like?' said Nora wryly, receiving a potent glare for her interruption.

'I just didn't want him putting words into my mouth. I prefer to speak for myself.' He squared his shoulders against the door, as if facing a firing squad. 'He's been at me for years to settle down and marry. He thinks it would make me a better CEO, more loyal to the idea of staying with the company for life. He doesn't want me making his mistake and having no one of the blood to carry on his legacy….'

'So he was keen for you to marry Hayley,' she dared to say thinly.

His head tipped back arrogantly. 'He knew that was never on the cards. Besides, it wouldn't have made any difference—she's no more of a blood relation to Scotty than I am.' The dry tone confirmed that he knew of the slanderous rumours.

Nora was beginning to picture a very demeaning scenario. She bit her lip. 'So when that newspaper came out, you told him we were engaged as a temporary way of getting him off your back and defusing the likelihood of a scandal…' she said hollowly.

Blake snibbed the lock on the door and walked across to where she stood, her slender back to his heavily laden desk.

'There is no scandal as far as I'm aware, and I certainly didn't tell Scotty that I'd asked you to marry me.'

'Oh!' Her cheeks flaming, she deflated into mortified silence. Sticking her hands into the deep pockets of the robe, she forced herself bravely on. 'You mean...he just assumed—'

'I mean that I merely said I was *thinking* of asking you to marry me. Scotty being Scotty immediately advanced to the next step. Modesty should forbid me to say it, but it doesn't seem to occur to him that any woman would refuse me....'

Nora's breathing had stopped somewhere in his first sentence. 'I—you—I don't understand,' she choked.

He reached up to gently finger the lapel of the robe, adjusting it where it folded across her breasts with meticulous hands. 'Don't you? And here I thought you might be feeling some of the things that I was feeling. It's all happened so fast for us, though, hasn't it? That's what makes it so scary,' he murmured, his eyes on his fingers rather than her pale face, and it came to her that he was as nervous as she was, that his hands weren't *quite* steady....

'It gives me a tiny inkling of what it must feel like for you when you're somewhere up high, at the mercy of an uncontrollable force inside you that seems to be pushing and pulling you at the same time.'

He described the feeling so exactly that Nora shivered. His eyes flicked up to her face, dark and intense.

'I've never asked a woman to marry me before, so I'm sorry if I'm not doing a very good job,' he said softly. 'We need each other, Nora.'

Her vulnerable mouth quivered, her golden eyes huge as they clung to his face, her hands stealing from her pockets to still his restless fingers.

'Y-you're talking about a sort of—marriage of convenience—?'

He looked thunderstruck. 'The hell I am! I'm obviously not doing this right...' He drew a breath, trying to curb his savage frustration. 'You told me once that I can be very overwhelming, so I've been trying to hold back, to give you a chance to feel comfortable with me, rather than helpless or overpowered—'

'Liar!' she said, exultation battling her disbelief. 'You've done your best to overwhelm me since the day we met!'

'Only because I was so overwhelmed myself,' he admitted with devastating sincerity. 'You always gave as good as you got.' His mouth quirked reminiscently. 'Better, sometimes...I admire that.' His voice dropped to a quiet, almost boyish, awkwardness. 'I admire *you*.'

The simple declaration was unbearably moving. 'Oh, Blake—'

His jaw clenched, as if she was daring to disagree. 'Life happens, Nora. Sometimes when you're least expecting it, fate throws a fantastic opportunity your way and you have to grab it with both hands, or risk losing it for ever.' He turned his hands over, interlacing his fingers with hers. 'I know you think I don't trust you, but it was myself I didn't trust, my own judgement that I had to question. I rarely act on impulse and yet with you I've been nothing but impulsive. But then, that's what love is, isn't it? Meeting someone you feel an instinctive connection with, someone who excites and surprises you, someone who rouses you to passion and makes you laugh, someone who makes you feel good about them and about yourself, who convinces you that the world is actually a wonderful place....'

Nora made a soft, inarticulate sound which he was quick to interpret as assent. He tucked her hands against his heart, a slight edge entering his voice as he talked fast, his face close to hers as he ruthlessly worked the most important deal of his life. 'Some people go through their whole lives never having that feeling about another person. I thought I would, too. Until I met you, Nora....'

'But we hardly know each other,' she murmured weakly.

He cupped her cheek, strong yet tender. 'Do you love me?'

'It's been less than two weeks—' she said, drowning in his eyes.

'And we've been lovers for almost as long. Do you want me?' Her lips turned to his palm. 'You know I do,' she relented.

'Then take the jump with me, Nora. Marry me.'

'Because you told your boss this morning that you were going to ask?' she said, from behind the last flimsy barrier of resistance.

Steel melted into a green-flecked tenderness. 'Actually I told him that day I came back from the beach that I'd met the woman I wanted to spend the rest of my life with…. He's been champing at the bit to meet you ever since, but I didn't want him to scare you off. I told my mother, too, when I asked her to pick you up. Thank God she kept that titbit from that big-mouthed sister of mine.'

'Blake, you didn't!' Her retrospective embarrassment was huge.

'If you take me, you get it all—my love, my children, my ever-loving, ever-annoying family, my interfering boss… I'll admit I come with plenty of extra baggage, but you need a lot of baggage for a long haul, Nora. And that's what it's going to be for us.'

'But still—' Her freckled face crinkled anxiously as she strove to be sensible in a world gone deliciously mad. '*A week and a half*…. We can't really know if we're compatible after such a short time….'

'That's what long engagements are for,' he said persuasively. 'With my ring on your finger we can have a proper courtship. You can move in with me when you're ready. Live with me for weeks, months, years—however long you need to feel safe in your choice of husband.'

His tone of martyred self-sacrifice made her want to laugh. 'As long as that ultimate choice is *you*,' she said wryly. He was so very big on offering her choices that had only one outcome!

'Yes…' He began to toy with the knot of the robe in a cunning way that made it suddenly fall apart. 'And, having said that, I'd naturally prefer that we married before our first baby is born,' he added, unable to resist the urge to negotiate better terms for himself. 'My mother is very tolerant of modern morality but Scotty would have fifty fits if his god-children were illegitimate.'

With a little giggle and a sly shimmy, Nora let the robe fall open. 'I suppose I can accept those terms.'

'You mean it?' he murmured, looking both delighted and indecently smug at his success.

'I love you; why wouldn't I love the idea of being your wife?' She laughed joyously as he whirled her into his extravagant embrace. 'And I especially love the idea that my indulgent new husband is going to let me drive his super-cool sports car whenever I want!'

Fortunately the champagne-fuelled celebrations had already begun down the hall and nobody heard the shrieks and growls that gradually dissolved in the sound of pure joy.

If you enjoyed what you just read,
then we've got an offer you can't resist!

Take 2 bestselling love stories FREE!
Plus get a FREE surprise gift!

Clip this page and mail it to Harlequin Reader Service®

IN U.S.A.
3010 Walden Ave.
P.O. Box 1867
Buffalo, N.Y. 14240-1867

IN CANADA
P.O. Box 609
Fort Erie, Ontario
L2A 5X3

YES! Please send me 2 free Harlequin Presents® novels and my free surprise gift. After receiving them, if I don't wish to receive anymore, I can return the shipping statement marked cancel. If I don't cancel, I will receive 6 brand-new novels every month, before they're available in stores! In the U.S.A., bill me at the bargain price of $3.80 plus 25¢ shipping & handling per book and applicable sales tax, if any*. In Canada, bill me at the bargain price of $4.47 plus 25¢ shipping & handling per book and applicable taxes**. That's the complete price and a savings of at least 10% off the cover prices—what a great deal! I understand that accepting the 2 free books and gift places me under no obligation ever to buy any books. I can always return a shipment and cancel at any time. Even if I never buy another book from Harlequin, the 2 free books and gift are mine to keep forever.

106 HDN DZ7Y
306 HDN DZ7Z

Name	(PLEASE PRINT)
Address	Apt.#
City	State/Prov.	Zip/Postal Code

Not valid to current Harlequin Presents® subscribers.

Want to try two free books from another series?
Call 1-800-873-8635 or visit www.morefreebooks.com.

* Terms and prices subject to change without notice. Sales tax applicable in N.Y.
** Canadian residents will be charged applicable provincial taxes and GST.
All orders subject to approval. Offer limited to one per household.
® are registered trademarks owned and used by the trademark owner and or its licensee.

PRES04R   ©2004 Harlequin Enterprises Limited

THREE MORE FREE BOOKS!